The Ecumenical Cruise
and Other
Three-Legged Chicken
Philosophy Tales

Walter Benesch

NONE
THE
LESS
PRESS

Kansas City

Printed in the United States of America
ISBN: 1-932053-07-7

Cover drawing by Sandy Jamieson
Book design by Z-N

Library of Congress Cataloging-in-Publication Data

Benesch, Walter, 1933-
 The ecumenical cruise and other three-legged chicken
philosophy tales
/ Walter Benesch.— 1st American ed.
    p. cm.
Includes bibliographical references.
 ISBN 1-932053-07-7 (hardcover : alk. paper)
 1. Philosophy—Fiction. 2. Didactic fiction, American. I. Title.
 PS3602.E663E27 2003
 813'.6—dc21

                            2003000764

NONE
THE
LESS
PRESS

http://www.nonethelesspress.com

10 9 8 7 6 5 4 3 2 1

The Ecumenical Cruise
and Other
Three-Legged Chicken
Philosophy Tales

Walter Benesch

Acknowledgements

Grateful acknowledgement is given to the following quarterlies and journals for their permisssion to reprint here the following stories: (U. of Kansas) The Kansas Quarterly VI, #1, "The Cup of Coffee"; (U. of British Columbia) Prism International, XIII, #9, "Helen Morley's Finger"; Pyramid, #4, "Metamorphosis" (as "Palingenesy").

Dedication

The Ecumenical Cruise and Other Three-Legged Chicken Philosophy Tales is dedicated to my sons, artists, and friends, Ilya and Oleg and their wonderful senses of humor!

Contents

Introduction: Three Legged Chickens

A Chinese philosopher in the Fourth Century BCE was known for his claim that 'a chicken has three legs'. He was not hallucinating nor are Chinese chickens different from the chickens of other nations. What the philosopher understood was that this 'third leg' was the mental leg or concept of 'chicken leg' that tells an observer that what he or she is seeing is a 'two-legged chicken.' This 'idea leg' is in the mind of the beholder, and it is a paradoxical synthesis of perception and conception, of seeing and not seeing, of the possible and the impossible.

Each story in *The Ecumenical Cruise and Other Three-Legged Chicken Philosophy Tales* is a three-legged chicken story that starts with statements found in philosophical and religious traditions from around the world, and then examines a 'mind egg' that such a chicken might conceivably lay. All similarities to poultry – living or dead – are purely coincidental.

Queen Vashti Goes to Heaven

Prologue

This story begins at the very beginning, which some would say is with *Genesis* 1:27-28 and the *first* description in the Hebrew Scriptures of the creation of human beings:

> "And God created man in his own image, in the image of God created he him: male and female created he them. And God blessed them: and God said unto them, Be fruitful and multiply..."

It then proceeds to the *second* description of human creation from *Genesis* 2:18-23:

> "...God said, It is not good that the man should be alone: I will make him a help meet for him...And God caused a deep sleep to fall upon the man, and he slept; and he took one of his ribs, and closed up the flesh instead thereof; and the rib which Jehovah God had taken from the man, made he a woman, and brought her unto the man. And the man said, This is now bone of my bones, and flesh of my flesh: and she shall be called Woman, because she was taken out of Man..."

From *Genesis*, it takes us to the *Book of Esther*, Chapters 1 and 2, where for the first time we encounter our story's heroine:

> "...in those days, when the king Ahasuerus sat on the throne of his kingdom...in the third year of his reign, he made a feast unto all his princes and his servants; the power of Persia and Media, the nobles and princes of the provinces, being before him; when he showed them the riches of his glorious kingdom and the honor

of his excellent majesty many days, even a hundred and fourscore days…Also Vashti the queen made a feast for the women in the royal house which belonged to king Ahasuerus. On the seventh day, when the heart of the king was merry with wine, he commanded…the seven chamberlains that minister in the presence of Ahasuerus the king, to bring Vashti the queen before the king with the crown royal, to show the peoples and the princes her beauty; for she was fair to look on. But the queen Vashti refused to come at the king's commandment by the chamberlains; therefore was the king very wroth, and his anger burned in him. Then the king said to the wise men…What shall we do unto the queen Vashti according to law because she hath not done the bidding of the king Ahasuerus…And Memucan answered before the law and the princes, Vashti the queen hath not done wrong to the king only, but also to all the princes, and to all the peoples that are in all the provinces of the king Ahasuerus. For this deed of the queen will come abroad unto all women, to make their husbands contemptible in their eyes, when it shall be reported…And this day will the princesses of Persia and Media who have heard of the deed of the queen say the like unto all the king's princes. So will there arise much contempt and wrath…let it be written among the laws of the Persians and the Medes…that Vashti come no more before king Ahasuerus; and let the king give her royal estate unto another that is better than she. And when the king's decree which he shall make shall be published through all his kingdom, all the wives will give to their husbands honor, both to great and small. And the saying pleased the king and the princes; and the king did according to the word of Memucan for he sent letters into all the king's provinces…After these things, when the wrath of king Ahasuerus was pacified, he remembered Vashti, and what she had done, and what was decreed against her. Then said the king's servants that ministered unto him, Let there be fair young virgins sought for the king, and let the king appoint officers in all the provinces of the kingdom that they may gather together all the fair young virgins unto the palace…and let the maiden that pleaseth the king be queen instead of Vashti. And the thing pleased the king and he did so."

It leaps the centuries from the Hebrew Scriptures to those of the Christians and to blessed St. Paul's first letter to the *Corinthians*, Chapters 11:7-9 and 14:33-35:

"…if a woman is not veiled, let her also be shorn; but if it is a shame to a woman to be shorn or shaven, let her be veiled. For a man indeed ought not to have his head veiled, forasmuch as he is the image and glory of God; but the woman is the glory of the man. For the man is not of the woman: but the woman of the man; for neither was the man created for the woman but the woman for the man: for this cause ought the woman to have a sign of authority on her head…"

"As in all the churches of the saints, let the women keep silence in the churches; for it is not permitted unto them to speak; but let them be in subjection, as also saith the law. And if they would learn anything, let them ask their own husbands at home; for it is shameful for a woman to speak in the church."

and continues in blessed St. Paul's first letter to *Timothy*, Chapter 2:11-15:

"Let a woman learn in quietness with all subjection. But I permit not a woman to teach, nor to have dominion over a man, but to be in quietness. For Adam was first formed, then Eve; and Adam was not beguiled, but the woman being beguiled hath fallen into transgression, but she shall be saved through her child-bearing, if they continue in faith and love and sanctification with sobriety."

Next, our story elaborates upon the tragic consequences of woman's weaker nature, described in that inspirational and prodigious work, the *Malleus Maleficarum*, a comprehensive and thorough study of and guide to the sources of witchcraft, written in the Sixteenth Century by two Dominican Inquisitors, Fr. Heinrich Kramer and Fr. James Sprenger under commission from Pope Innocent VIII. Here at last we learn the true significance of the creation of Eve from Adam's rib, as these two pious Friars explain *"Why it is that Women are chiefly addicted to Evil Superstitions".* These two Dominican 'warriors of truth' explain quite clearly that women are not only weaker in mind and body, as experience 'clearly shows', but they are also by nature 'imperfect animals', for they were formed from a 'bent rib', which by its curved shape is always bent in a 'contrary direction' to the man. Born with this fundamental defect, it is clear that women will deceive and demonstrate a propensity to witchcraft.[1]

After the Christian texts, the path of our story winds through the *Glorious Koran*, which in *Surah* IV #34 informs us quite clearly that Allah placed men in charge of women, for they were made to be so, and because it is the responsibility of men with their goods and property to support women. It is the responsibility of women to be obedient and chaste just as Allah made them so. If, however, a woman is rebellious or disobedient, she should be sent to a separate bed and scourged. If she then sees the error of her ways, she should not be punished further. Allah is ever High, Exalted, Great![2] And in *Surah* XXXIII #59, the Prophet was cautioned that all the women folk, wives and daughters of believers should wrap themselves in their cloaks whenever they leave the dwelling.[3]

From the Western Greek, and beyond the Near Eastern texts of the Jew, Christian and Muslim, our introduction expands to include the biological knowledge of the great Aristotle, who clearly explains in his *Generation of Animals* that just as both normal and deformed offspring are born sometimes to deformed parents, even so is it the case that the children of females are male and sometimes female. And he explains that the reason for this is that the female is in essence a deformed male. The source of this difference is that 'menstrual discharge' is really semen, but in an impure condition, for it lacks the principle of *soul which is the one critical ingredient necessary for the production of the male child*.[4]

From the mystic Eastern World, our introduction incorporates as well the insights of the law book of the Hindu, the eternal *Laws of Manu*:

> "Through their passion for men, through their mutable temper, through their natural heartlessness, they become disloyal towards their husbands, however carefully they may be guarded in this world. …[When creating them] Manu allotted to women [a love of their] bed, [of their] seat, and [of] ornament, impure desires, wrath, dishonesty, malice, and bad conduct. For women no [sacramental] rite [is performed] with sacred texts, thus the law is settled: women [who are] destitute of strength and destitute of [the knowledge of] Vedic texts, [are as impure as] falsehood [itself]."[5]

It couples this insight with the Buddhists' understanding of suffering, detailed in the *Blindfold Jataka*:

> "The nature of the woman is hard to know,
> 'Tis like the ways in water of the fish.
> Lies are to them as truth, and truth as lies…
> She bandits are they, cruel and malign,
> And hard and fickle…"[6]

Finally our introduction comes to rest in the Christian Gnostic *Gospel of Thomas*, with that greatest of all miracles performed by Jesus, the transformation of Mary Magdalene:

> "Simon Peter says to them: Let Mary [Magdalene] go out from our midst, for women are not worthy of Life! Jesus says: See, I will draw her so as to make her male so that she also may become a living spirit like you males. For every woman who has become male will enter the kingdom of heaven."[7]

She was not initially clear on how it started…sitting there in that crowded lounge waiting for her flight. Someone had announced over the public address system that it would be a long trip and, because of travel restrictions and immigration regulations, no food or drink could be served during the flight, therefore the last refreshments would be offered in the waiting area. Passengers were urged to avail themselves of the juice and snacks that would be distributed shortly.

Presently, a group of stewards in identical light blue uniforms, with thin, well trimmed mustaches and short sideburns, had come through the lounge pushing carts stacked high with sandwiches – ham or beef for the carnivores, ground broccoli paste for the vegetarians – plus pitchers of what seemed an endless supply of tomato juice for filling and refilling glasses.

She hadn't been hungry, so she had simply put the sandwich in her bag and, though thirsty, had given her juice to the little boy sitting next to her who had managed to dump his down the front of his sailor suit. While his mother mopped him up with a napkin, she held her glass steady for the lad so he could drink without further disaster.

The room was very warm and exuded a thick smell of soap, expensive perfume, disinfectant, and sweat. The flight had apparently been delayed – but at least everyone had a chair or seat of some kind, with a space for a small bag that could be pushed under it. They were informed that later these bags would need to be deposited in the overhead luggage compartments. After the sparse refreshment, individuals already exhausted from waiting and dulled by the poor air in the room started to doze – singly or in groups, as parents shared their laps with infants. She wasn't particularly tired, but resisting sleep was like trying not to yawn when others about you are yawning. Slowly her chin dipped toward her chest, and she wondered in half-sleep, "…so this is what it means to die and sit waiting for one's flight to heaven…I hope there'll be more room and fresh air there – when I get there – than there is in this place…"

Her eyes closed. The thin flame of consciousness burned so low that even time itself seemed to have stopped. But some corner of her mind on the rim of awareness was whispering something…something important…she just couldn't make it out…a memory…a remembering…and as her curiosity cleared her mind fog a bit she thought she recalled having been in this room waiting for this flight before…sitting near the "Departure Gate" sign…no…not there…or maybe not 'just there'…over there by the counter where the carts with the snacks had been loaded and launched…and there…where that potted palm was standing…certainly…she could remember that palm with the hanging, broken fronds…it had been very important for some reason…a desert…had it been in a desert…had she been in a desert?

It made no sense…but the images were becoming sharper…she could almost see herself sitting in different chairs all around the room. The same room and always full of people, but different people…or maybe not…she thought she had seen some of them before…like the mother whose little boy had spilled his juice, she'd been there…over by the palm and without the little boy…she had been older too, more a grandmother than a mother.

Although she was wide awake now, she still hadn't opened her eyes, concerned that the clarity of her remembering, as in a dream, would not tolerate the light. Was this what death was like? Memories…but what queer memories…of all the places she'd sat in a room where she was sure she'd been dozens maybe hundreds of times before? This thought was like the lifting of a floodgate. More than memories of the room…memories of life and lives came rushing back. She tried to reject the thought, even as it occurred to her…I've lived before and died and lived and died…and this means I've never made the flight!

Something else, her memory prompted, as her mind quickened its pace…she'd always drunk the tomato juice. She remembered tasting the sandwiches once or twice…they were made with some sort of flat bread and rubbery meat or vegetable paste. She'd never cared for them and couldn't recall ever entirely consuming one. But with the juice it was different. She remembered her thirst in this room…she was always thirsty…always drank the juice. Only this time, because the little boy had spilled his, she'd given him hers. The juice! She was positive her memories had something to do with not having drunk the juice!

She opened her eyes. The room was empty! Only the chairs and the palm tree remained. A steward was standing in front of her with a glass of tomato juice in his right hand and a sandwich in the other. "Here, you'd best drink this. The flight is long and, because of travel restrictions and immigration regulations, there will be no refreshments served on board."

She jumped up and so startled him that the glass fell out of his hand. "No, no juice! Where's everyone gone? Has the flight left? Have I missed it?"

"No, no, your flight will be departing momentarily. Here, let me fetch you some juice. The flight is long and due to travel restrictions and immigration regulations there will be no refreshments served on board."

But now she was awake…felt alive though she knew she was dead…for before coming here she had been the center of attraction at the service where…where…and now, even with her eyes open, the visions and dream fragments began again. With a shock, she realized that she'd always been the center of attraction at a string of funerals and memorials and last rites…some in forests, some in fields, some in cathedrals, churches, homes, on pyres…though the cast of characters standing around varied…sometimes they were black, other times white or yellow. Sometimes they were weeping, sometimes rejoicing, sometimes yawning. Sometimes there were children, sometimes not…but she was always the center of attention…the dearly beloved in a long hall of passings and mumblings and chantings. Then the sorrowful mourners were replaced by cuddling, holding, scolding, patting hands…sudden lights and sounds, the feel of the hard earth, the smell of hay…choking…screams…unable to get her breath…

The steward returned with a fresh glass of juice, and was accompanied by a supervisor whose mustaches were complemented by a short goatee and longer sideburns. She again refused the juice, certain now it was a drink, not to facilitate her flight to paradise, but to deaden her memory…for her there had never been a flight to paradise…"No! No…No!"

The supervisor quietly insisted, "But the flight is a long one and due to travel restrictions and immigration regulations there will be no refreshments served on board."

She would have none of it! "Let me out!" she suddenly commanded, and from a center someplace deep within her being a powerful voice welled up. "I am the Queen! I am Queen Vashti!"

The steward paled and the proffered glass of juice slipped again from his hand and smashed on the floor. His superior vanished behind the flight gate door and returned moments later with a tall, blond gentleman in a spotless white uniform with gold epaulettes and embroidery of most marvelous and intricate design. A brilliant gold stripe ran down each trouser leg, terminating in his small, golden boots. His mustaches and sideburns, like those of the superior, were blond, but fuller and more stern above his slightly longer blond goatee.

She assumed it was Memucan, the minister who suggested to Ahasuerus that his wife had committed an unpardonable sin that would make him the laughingstock of the Persians and Medes and lead to women around the kingdom viewing their husbands as mere mortals.

"Memucan, you scoundrel, how did you get here with your hair all blonded up and your eyebrows dyed?"

"Madam," he unctioned, "if you will follow me please." He turned and led her, not to the flight gate, but to another door through which they entered a spacious office carpeted and wallpapered in gold. At a golden desk before a golden sun illumined window sat a second figure, whose entire uniform was gold. He rose to greet her.

"Madam, you are distraught. It would be best if you drank your tomato ju…"

"I'm not interested in tomato juice! I demand an explanation!"

"Madam, the flight is indeed a long one and due to travel restrictions and the regulations imposed by immigration…"

"There is no flight, and you know it and I know it!"

"But Madam, the tomato juice is of a superior quality, processed from fresh, organically grown tomatoes and touched in processing only by the hands of young, virgin tomato pickers. And I think…"

"To hell with your tomato juice and virgin pluckers…I am Queen Vashti and I demand to know what's going on! I recognize you now, and all the gold plate doesn't fool me…you are Memucan, that worthless and ill-begotten son of a sheep tick, and advisor to my addle-brained, drunken husband, King Ahasuerus! I suppose he can depose me and take my jewels, furs and furniture…evict me from the palace with only the clothes on my back, but…"

"Madam, your highness, I really believe that a small glass of tomato juice, perhaps with a touch of vodka…"

"If you bring in one more small glass of tomato juice, with or without vodka, I will empty its entire contents up your left nostril! Now, where is he?"

"Who, Madam?"

"Ahasuerus, you idiot, that pompous, posturing pile of camel poop excuse for a king, who else? Ahasuerus, who thinks he can replace me with a bunch of nymphets and pixies…who else?"

"Ahasuerus is in paradise, Madam, and cannot be summoned from there. I am not Memucan. He too is in heaven, where you might also be if you would just drink your tomato juice…perhaps a sip…"

"You really don't think much of your left nostril, do you? Bring the juice and lean back…and if you're not Memucan, who are you and how did that pair of rogues get into paradise?"

"I am Theodorus Maximus of the third rank. Your worthy husband and his worthy minister left on an earlier flight some time ago, just as you could now be leaving if…that is…well…if…"

"Fine, we're through with your tomato juice fixation. Now we're ready for some explaining. And I don't mean from a third rate Maximus. I want to see whoever is in charge here, even if it is one of the gods!"

"No! That's not possible. I will see if Michael or Gabriel is available. Now, if you would just relax for a moment and drink…I mean think quieting and wholesome thoughts, I will see what I can do."

Hardly had he left Vashti impatiently beating time with her foot, when a door she had not noticed before opened and what was either a bird-man or an angel entered. He was at least eight feet tall, clad in a white robe that glowed with an iridescent sheen. Long silver locks flowed about a pair of sharp blue eyes and melded into a long, white, immaculately trimmed beard. Great wings gently and quietly quivered as he walked – as though they resented his sandals touching the floor. The voice was soft and soothing, the smile radiant and warm – only the blue ice in the eyes remained cold and penetrating.

"My dear Queen Vashti, I have so long awaited the pleasure of making your acquaintance. Of course, from afar I have observed…ah…your troubles…but those are past and you have joined us here on the flight deck at last…"

But Vashti cut him off before he could offer her tomato juice. "Something is wrong here, and I think I now know what it is…and it starts with that damned tomato juice…whether squeezed by virgins or chimpanzees. One drink of that stuff and the memory goes 'whoof'…all gone! Can't remember a thing. Fortunately, this time around I didn't drink it. And I stress 'this time' because it is clear to me that I've been drugged here before! I show up for this flight, time after time, and I get doped and dumped back into some uterus to be reborn and start the whole thing over again! I never make the flight, yet your flunky, Gluteus Maximus, informs me that my worthless husband and his sycophantic minister left for paradise a long time ago! Now, you tell me what's going on…I don't get on board and those scoundrels do? And another thing, this didn't begin yesterday. You've been dumping me back for centuries and every time drugged with virgin tomato juice, au naturel. Off I go. With no memory…too dumb to realize each time that I'd been here before and before and before…and always coming back from your flight deck for more. Nope! No! And if you try to touch me and force your damned tomato juice down my throat, I promise to scream and bite and punch my way out of here to whatever is out there…to break out of here! Do you hear me? To tell people everywhere how they are being duped and recycled with a phony flight scam which robs your memory but never departs!"

"Well, now, I think you and I can calmly discuss what seems to you to be a problem with our modus operandi here…" The voice increased its unctuousness by seventy-five percent, the smile provided enough warmth that Vashti could have warmed her toes in its glow. But there was no warming of toes for the enraged Queen.

"Ok, begin...explain to me what's going on before I leave this room and start my crusade against your fraudulent operation!"

"Now, now. I think, my dear Queen, and with all respect to you and your husband, whom I also admire...such a crusade would not be in your best interests or those of humanity at large. You see, your situation applies to only one-half and a bit more of the human race. We do accept men and boys on our flights. Of course, we have immigration restrictions that apply to...shall we say...um...an...androgynous entities...and...others. Others, shall we say, like...a yourself...ah..."

"...ah...women you mean!"

"Well, in a sense, yes. It is clearly demonstrated in scriptures from Buddhist to Confucian, to Hindu, to Jew, to Muslim, to Christian that the female soul is smaller, sometimes almost non-existent, incomplete, and generally of a more servile nature. Not the sort of soul that is really fitted for paradise, but instead a biological soul, which is best adapted to bearing, birthing, and mothering. In fact, it is indispensable for bearing and birthing, as even sainted Thomas Aquinas maintained. It is a soul critical to the production not only of great theologians, priests, philosophers, imams, ayatollahs, scientists, warriors, rajahs, and other rulers, but also essential to the preservation and survival of the species. This, my dear Queen, is your and your sisters' great achievement and accomplishment. Why, paradise pales when compared with the joy of bearing and birthing those tender innocents who will be the next generation's leaders! If you feel that you must march out and demonstrate...then speak to your sisters and tell them how lucky they are to find their paradise here on earth in the fertile processes of giving birth and being reborn!"

The diamond-blue eyes sparkled at the logic of this most reasonable of arguments.

"Dromedary pucky, that's the stupidest thing I've ever heard!! You mean men, and only men, get to heaven?"

"Well, and boys too, and an occasional gallant stallion. But...not all men and boys qualify, as wise Plato was clearly aware. Men who are cowards in battle, for example, are reborn as women and lose their opportunity, and transvestites too...and, as our beloved St. Paul noted, men whose hair exceeds a certain length. No, no, we do have standards."

"And women...no women are admitted...and so are condemned to rebirth as women for ever and ever?"

"Ah...that's...um...quite true, but if one contemplates the whole picture, not just from the perspective of the joy of bearing and birthing, but also considers...um...the...ah...the problems it would create in heaven...I mean, look about you. Now you, your Majesty, are a woman of great experience and insight, particularly now that you remember so much of your past. How have things been on earth from Eve and Cleopatra to what's her name with the blue dress? Nothing but problems! Do we want that in heaven? Do you want that in heaven? Think about what it would mean if we introduced...ah...you know...a sort of temptation into the heavenly chambers with their choirs eternally singing glorious hosannas in the highest...the loss of tone, the changes in pitch...no...no! Um...you must admit that it would never do. And here on earth, who would give birth to new generations of choir boys...and of course their mothers, if women were to fly off into the clouds? Ah...the very thought causes one to tremble!"

"Pfui...I don't want to tremble, I want to throw up! Who is responsible for this assbackwards way of running the universe? That's what I want to know! What nincompoop figured this one out?" Queen Vashti stormed now, for she was a proud and a haughty woman and the fear of God was not in her.

"Well, since we are being quite frank with one another...surely you must have learned even centuries ago among the Medes and Persians that in the beginning God made man, and then from one of Adam's ribs formed a woman, Eve. It has been so from the beginning. And on the seventh day the Creator rested...and as a matter of fact is still resting, which is why we don't raise our voices here, and certainly another reason for not permitting women, who are generally garrulous, gossipy, and harping, into heaven to create incessant chatter and wake the Creator from his peaceful slumbers."

"By the sacred upper eyelid of Tiamat's third eye! You believe that Adam's rib stuff?"

"Not only do we believe it, we know it to be true for we have seen the process reversed. This I have witnessed with my own eyes. Not often, mind you, but often enough to convince."

"What? You mean women turned back into men's ribs again? Nonsense!"

"Not really women, but one woman in particular...a miracle performed by no lesser a being than the Creator's own son who chose, in addition to his twelve disciples (for even Judas was included after a stint of community service as water boy in the bathhouses of Herculaneum)...I say that, in addition to the twelve who were to form his heavenly team, Jesus also wanted Mary Magdalene to join them. Of course the apostles were rightly opposed to such a thing...until Jesus convinced them it would be all right if he were to turn her into a man...that is by transforming her into a rib and then providing the rib with a rib cage, testosterone, and other...ah...male accoutrements...which I am sure I need not list here for one of your experience."

"You do actually believe that rib stuff, don't you? The old guy must have been sniffing something when he thought that one up...you mean this poor woman, Mary, got hocus-pocused into spareribs?"

"That's rather crudely put...but in essence, yes, and she, I mean he, is one of the star athletes in most heavenly competitions."

"Well, not me! I want to see the Chief!"

At this the diamond-blue eyes grew colder and sharper, as a solution gradually suggested itself to their owner. He, with a capital 'H', had slept long enough, almost seven thousand years, counting from the creation of Adam. So, if He were to be awakened now at the summons of this female, squawking about getting into heaven and making a mess of the order there, shamelessly tempting the heavenly hosts right and left...He might with a single blinding flash of lightning either terminate her miserable existence...or...and this was the risky part...clarify what was really a tricky theological dilemma. You see, the Archangel Michael, like the rest of the senior angels, knew there were two versions of the creation, so to speak. At the time God had created humanity He was probably a bit confused, which was not surprising seeing that He had been around forever. In the original creation He had made men and women in

His own image as male and female. This had raised the horrible fact of the Deity's own androgynous nature being passed on to His human creation.

Fortunately, God had fallen asleep almost immediately thereafter, before He could take too close an interest in the mess He had generated for the heavenly host who had been all male for eons. If this androgynous creation that was equally male and female were left to stand, the heavenly host would have to start accommodating chatterboxes and gossiping breast feeders, and this in a place where the heavenly host consumed only liquid ambrosia, and where the urinal had ably served everyone for ages past and would serve them in ages to come. The construction of equal but separate rest rooms and sleeping facilities would take longer than the entire six days of creation itself. No! It could not be, and so, while God slept, the heavenly hosts had tampered a bit with the texts. They couldn't alter the creation itself, of course, but they were in charge of setting up provisions for carrying out the divine 'handiwork' from day to day – shaping the immigration regulations for the after-life, keeping paradise orderly and clean. And with the deity sleeping, they could, as Raphael had suggested, rewrite certain texts and put them into the fertile minds of prophets and priests as revelations that clearly indicated what God had intended to do, rather than what he may have seemed to have done. And that bit with Jesus, about whose ancestry Muslims, Jews, and Christians still argued, had been the ultimate vindication of all their efforts to keep paradise safe and clean. It was indeed a great miracle when he was able to turn Mary Magdalene first into a rib and then into a man named Josephus – Bubba, to his friends – and so take her/him back to heaven without any danger of upsetting the existing order of things, or introducing unseemly sexual activities into paradise.

Now here was…this…this…the first woman to remember her past, who was not just unhappy, but determined to do something about it! It was clear that even if he grabbed her and made her drink her tomato juice, she would waken the deity, whose sleep all had noticed was getting lighter of late. She might just do it…and then…what about the changes in the text? Maybe He wouldn't notice or couldn't recall what He had done long ago. He was bound to be forgetful after so long a time. Maybe they could claim the first creation story was a misprint? It might work, unless He managed to catch His reflection someplace in a comet or an exploding star. In any case she would have to be silenced, but how? She wasn't having any tomato juice. Was there perhaps another, possibly less violent, resolution of her demands?

"Well, my dear Queen Vashti, as I reflect now upon your situation and your meritorious years of service as mothers and wives of generations of kings and popes and patriarchs and princes and ayatollahs and imams..."

"Don't try to con me with your 'dear queen' gibberish...nor prate about kings and popes and princes...after Ahasuerus, that malformed, misogynic magnum of mirth, threw me out, there were three sheepherders in succession and one sheep!"

"That was an oversight and we corrected it at once!"

"Yes, corrected it when the wolves ate both of us...and 'meritorious services' my foot...virgin sacrifice to four different volcanoes and one sea monster. Nero's childhood sweetheart, wives of six maharajas, one of whom thought he was a water buffalo and behaved accordingly...the other five were just insane. Purdah bagged bride, slave, and plaything of mullahs, imams, sultans, and emirs. Mistress of three popes including the illustrious Alessandro who never washed his socks...of course he never took his boots off either. Foot-bound concubine to four mandarins and one half-size, yin-yangy warlord who found foot binding particularly erotic when extended to the knees. Burned twice at the stake for witchcraft, scalped four times, traded for beads and a basket of bananas to a Swahili chieftain who wanted a royal footstool, flayed, flogged, prostituted, destituted, circumscribed, circumcised, died in childbirth twenty-seven times, smothered as a 'female baby' in China, Japan, Arabia, and Madagascar! Meritorious service...you can have it!"

"Ahem, as I was saying, your Majesty, I...we...have carefully considered your...ah...contributions and believe that they possess great merit, and we will begin the necessary preparations at once for transforming you into a man...first into a noble and regal rib and then into an illustrious rib cage. Do you have a man's name that particularly appeals to you?"

"Into a rib, then into a rib cage then into a barbecue? No thanks, I'll enter heaven on my own with my own ribs and rib cage and no 'male accoutrements'!"

With her cold rejection of the generous offer to make her into a man, Queen Vashti, in her wanton pride, seemed to have chosen a course from which there could be no turning back. Of course, for Michael there was a certain risk involved in his alternative plan to accommodate her. To admit the Queen to heaven would not be a problem if she were completely covered. He would arrange with the guard at the sleeping Deity's vaulted chambers to let her into the anteroom, and, based on his astute observations of her lack of self control, he had no doubt that she would screech and scream until even God could no longer slumber. Then, if the Deity did not slay her at once, which was highly probable, for He was always in a bad mood for a couple of centuries when He woke up…but, assuming He didn't cinderize her at once, they would need to bring the corrected creation story to His attention and explain the measures they had undertaken to preserve the order that had always existed in paradise. Then perhaps a turn around the gardens, the playing fields and the tracks, where He could see how wise this decision had been as He watched the men and boys at their athletic contests. How proud He would be!

As it was thought, so was it acted upon. Queen Vashti was placed on a special flight. No tomato juice, no sandwiches, and, though she had protested at first to wearing a black canvas burqa that covered her from head to floor, she finally acquiesced when told it was an unavoidable condition for entering the deity's presence.

In paradise, as the Archangel Michael and Queen Vashti prepared to enter the anteroom of the Deity's slumber chambers, it became quickly apparent that the Deity's slumbering was over and that even the sound of the opening of the outer door was enough to awaken Him…for when they entered the outer chamber, the door to the inner slid noiselessly back into a huge cloud bank, and a great, blinking, sort of sleep-sodden Eye opened on the top of a giant pyramid and glared down at them. It was clear that the Deity was in a foul mood.

"Your Awesome Awesomeness…" Michael started.

"Why are you dragging a sack of potatoes in here?" thundered that greatest of all voices. The staring Eye had stopped blinking now and was staring at Vashti in her canvas burqa.

"I'm not a sack of potatoes, your Omnipotence, I am Queen Vashti, and they made me put this bag on just like they have been messing with me and my sisters ever since you did that dumb trick with Adam's rib!" And without further ado, and to the horror of the angels great and small who had gathered to watch a cinderizing, Vashti the Queen tore off the black burqa and stood unabashed and unadorned before the Almighty, clad only in the simple shift that had been her burial dress!

Everyone stepped back! Some lesser angels fled so as not to have their feathers singed by what was now sure to happen. The Eye grew angry and reddened, as though it was about to burst into flame. More angels left, including some of the members of the chamber guard. Just as it seemed that a cataclysmic eruption was set to begin another Eye opened at the top of the pyramid and stared intently at the Queen – not angry but puzzled. Now both Eyes stared, closed, blinked, closed again. All the angels and Queen Vashti held their breath. Finally, with the Eyes still closed, a Voice, almost a yawn, asked, "So…what's all this about?"

The Eyes opened again and Vashti, undaunted, seized her chance. In a torrent of anger and scorn she related the pain and suffering and the destruction that the 'creation' had become. She told the rib story. Upon hearing it the Voice made muffled sounds as though it were struggling not to laugh. For the first time both Eyes had a strange sparkle in them. And when Vashti told the story about the 'smaller souls' that women were supposed to have, and recounted the names of the kings and princes and popes and priests and mandarins and maharajahs and ayatollahs and sultans and their misdeeds…the twinkle in the Eyes grew somber. And when Vashti related how women could get to heaven only by becoming men, otherwise they were given tomato juice and sent home, the Voice was angry and summoned all the Archangels and the still greater angels with six rows of wings and those with ten for an accounting of the Queen's story. And the angels explained the necessity of keeping temptation out of heaven, the costs of separate rest rooms and sleeping quarters, the scandal that would surely follow, and the value of preserving heaven's order where certain genders of men and angels alone could really...

Suddenly, the two Eyes winked at one another...and to this day no one, angel or man, can explain how they managed to do this and it is taken simply as further proof that God's ways are not our ways. The wink was followed by a great cosmic swoosh, and then a swish and then a cosmic yelp that reverberated for days throughout the heavenly vaults and chambers, and on the playing fields where the heavenly hosts were at their games.

Then the voice said to Vashti, "Welcome," and placed her in charge of editing all the world's scriptures, both from the past and as they might be written in the future. And she was made the *Queen of Revelations and Omens and Signs* and given an infinite supply of Band-Aids® to take with her as she traveled through the heavenly realms.

This is why when you meet angels today, or see them pictured in books and paintings, they no longer have beards or mustaches or sideburns or steroidal biceps and abs, and their long locks, if not feminine, certainly have an androgynous wave to them. And this is why one need no longer be a male to enter paradise, and why even cowards in battle make it, and transvestites too get in, and why Jesus was ordered to shave.

Amen

The Cup of Coffee

William Shakespeare's Jaques in *As You Like It* sagely comments that really...

> "All the world's a stage,
> And all the men and women merely players:
> They have their exits and their entrances;
> And one man in his time plays many parts..."
> (Act II, Scene 7)

However, in King Sudraka's *The Toy Cart*, Charudatta insists that some parts are better than others and from this difference evil follows:

> "A man poor is a man ashamed;
> A man ashamed is a man without dignity.
> Frustration follows insult, despair follows frustration,
> Indecision follows despair.
> From this small root, all man's evils grow."
> (Act I)[1]

Grace Norton and her very best friend, widows of seventy-two years and one morning, are discussing the pending funeral services for Margaret Bolton's second husband. It is Grace's apartment and Grace likes her coffee filtered. As the water warms, the brown scent of freshly ground beans overwhelms the small kitchen.

Grace sits at the kitchen table, her rather dramatic backside to the refrigerator. She leans her arms on the table, the full weight of her ponderous upper torso coarse against the cant. The pungent coffee vapors take her in full strength, topping the little gray mustache to titillate her hair-hung nostrils. Moist droplets pearl anticipation patterns on the gently flexing tongue in the half-opened mouth. Grace's mouth is always half apart, but she breathes through her nose. She is not a 'mouth breather' as some of her friends insist behind her back.

Grace's very best friend, as guest, is granted the coffee ritual. She is a tall, thin woman, quite gray now, with a fine furrow slightly to the right of the center of her forehead. Here a small perspiration droplet emerges occasionally to make its way slowly down to the tip of her nose and vanish in a sandy layer of face powder that conceals the flat surface shine. Grace's best friend is fond of fresh milled coffee too, but it is a luxury that she can afford only when visiting.

Both women are sorry for Margaret Bolton, though they do not conceal in their sympathy their conviction that for a second marriage she might have selected more wisely.

Grace Norton's cousin Alice grew up in the same neighborhood as he, went to school with him. Alice has assured Grace on numerous occasions that even as a child he was an exhibitionist, a "constructionist" who entertained other children by "throwing his arms out of joint and tossing his head back and forth like a chicken when he should have been studying."

The best friend wonders if there will be an open-coffin ceremony? Always depressing and yet somehow appropriate to the great sorrow of final leave taking...

"Besides," Grace interrupts her, "when I first met him, he frightened me with those hideous lips of his. My cousin Alice says he sucked his thumb all the time as a boy and that's why his lips got so large and curled up...and when he talked they looked like sausages. He did it to frighten us. He was an exhibitionist!"

The best friend, sitting across from Grace, stirs her coffee. She admits sagely that she was appalled when she learned that Margaret Bolton was to marry a freak...a man who made his living by turning himself inside out!

The Cup of Coffee

This was indeed the case. He could, by deflating his lungs and forcing his inner organs upward with the abdominal muscles, turn his organism back upon itself. The skeletal structure remained fixed, but the eyes rolled inward. The ears disappeared in their cavities. The nostrils crept to the roof of the mouth – the pink and mucoused tongue serving then as a nose. The navel retreated. The stomach and duodenum, plus about two feet of small intestine emerging like a necktie, were suspended cautiously from his teeth so their weight would not rupture the tender tissue. His toes curled around his heels. His fingers, bone and flesh, slid up beneath the veined skin of his hands, vanished in the blunt and back-bent palms. Rumor had it that his anus swallowed…but no one ever knew, as Grace said, because when he performed he wore a pair of clean white shorts with a crimson "M" for Margaret on them.

The best friend fills Grace's cup and empties the last two teaspoonfuls into her own. She would enjoy a second cup but it is Grace's coffee and Grace's apartment. She would never have the courage to grind a few additional beans. Grace always measures them out and specifies the amount of water. It is just enough for three and one-quarter cups. The best friend's thoughts wander again to the open coffin. All the funerals in her family are open-coffin affairs. It is a tradition. She fully expects it herself…but she doesn't know whether Margaret thinks much of tradition. And Margaret is wealthy. Maybe…

"I could never figure out why she married him in the first place. George left her well off after their settlement. She certainly didn't need to pick up a freak!"

Grace removes the lid from the container of beans on the table and the smell emerges virile and eager. The best friend stares at the brown, fat beans. She has instant coffee at home, of course, but not beans and a mill and…Grace's husband left a number of lesser stocks and bonds and an insurance policy, which pays for beans and a car and a small but expensive apartment. All she has is her Social Security pension. There isn't much for extras. She baby-sits several nights a week when she can for the neighbors. In her building they all drink instant coffee.

Grace closes the lid and the best friend moves her attention from the container to Grace's rings. If one has things of value, like rings and bracelets, then the only way to assure that they...whatever they call the people who work on things like dead people...the only way to assure they don't steal them is with an open-coffin ceremony where everybody would notice if they were gone...

Grace spoons her coffee against her waiting tongue. "Of course he wasn't very old either, I'm told. Much younger than Margaret. But that sort of thing is exhausting. I certainly wouldn't do it for all the money in the world, turn myself inside out in front of all those people!"

The best friend is not sure...would she turn herself inside out for all that money? Naturally she would require more than a pair of white shorts with a red letter for Margaret. It might be so embarrassing...would an open-coffin funeral be embarrassing?

"Some people are born exhibitionists. There's no way to help them. I just feel sorry for Margaret, that's all." Grace has the lid off the beans again.

The best friend raises her eyes from her empty cup to the chocolate-colored jewels. For a moment the thought flits by that Grace is tormenting her...it is immediately swallowed by the overpowering bean smell. Why do beans smell so much better than the cheaper instant she buys?

Grace rises to get a glass of water. The chair grinds against the kitchen tiles. Her cup is half full and half warm. The best friend doesn't notice...turn herself inside out for all the money in the world?

"And," Grace wipes her mouth on the red napkin, "of course that's what finally killed him. Like the paper said. He turned himself inside out and had a stroke and they couldn't get him back right so he died. There in public! Margaret must have been terribly embarrassed. Especially when people had paid seventy-five dollars a seat and he was only halfway through the show. Of course I wasn't there. I saw him twice before and that's enough for me. Once in New York and once in Los Angeles. Besides, seventy-five dollars a seat! He was famous, but seventy-five is still seventy-five! Once you've seen that sort of thing a couple of times, it's enough, don't you think?"

Grace finishes her coffee and goes to the bedroom to dress. It is time to get ready. The best friend clears the table...would a couple of times be enough? If somebody'd made a movie... might she have seen that twice? Of course it wouldn't be the same...

Two beans snuggle near the creamer where Grace has dropped them...she certainly wouldn't miss them? The best friend places them one at a time back into the container. She unplugs the mill and runs a moistened finger through the powdery residue beneath the blades, wipes it gently across her tongue...how good the bitter dust is...

Satori at the Doughnut Stop

Prologue

The early Greek philosopher, Parmenides of Elea, insisted that what is *is* what it is, and what is not *is not* and can never be *ised*. For him *thought* and *being* and *language* all reflect the same and unchanging *isness* of the world. Thus anyone who believes *something* could come from *nothing* or that *something* could become *nothing* is befuddled indeed.[1]

The Buddhist philosopher Nagarjuna rejected the entire *something/nothing dichotomy* and argued instead that everything and anything *is, is not, both is and is not,* and finally *neither is nor is not*. For Nagarjuna all is *emptiness* and even *emptiness* is *empty*.[2]

But, proposed the medieval Christian, Nicholas of Cusa, it was his God who made *nothing* into *something* by naming it and calling *nothing* forth to become *something*. Thus it is possible, or was in the beginning, to get *something* from *nothing*.[3]

A doughnut hole and a slightly rancid yeast doughnut, positioned on a high shelf in the back room of the Doughnut Stop for a late break by the second shift dishwasher, were earnestly discussing the merits and possibilities of *nothingness* versus *emptiness*. The doughnut was of the opinion that *nothingness* was clearly more important and relevant to the way things are, for *nothingness* derived its nature and essence from *something* and *somethingness*. And since *something* always has mass and occupies space, then *nothing* and *nothingness* can indicate only the negation of *something* and the lack of *somethingness* respectively. Thus it would be impossible to speak of *nothing* or know *nothing* except one knew *something* and then either denied it or forgot it. Besides, as even young doughnuts fresh from the deep fryer realize, one can neither get *something* from *nothing* nor *nothing* from *something* – and so *nothing* always remains a kind of cancelled reflection of *something*.

The hole, who understood the direction its colleague was taking and also the implications for its own nature, then asked, "But is a hole then not *something*? Have holes no claim on being? Could one not command another, and quite intelligibly I might add, to *create a hole*, to *dig a hole*, to *locate a hole* or, God forbid, even to *fix a hole*? Surely, then, a hole is *something*! But if this is the case, would not the absence of a hole be *nothing*? And, of course, if the absence of a hole were *nothing*, it would mean that without its hole a doughnut too would be *nothing*! In this case then it is not the doughnut – really *nothing* – that gives the hole its identity, but rather the hole that preserves the doughnut from becoming *nothing*! I have the feeling that this is not what you had intended when you began, but there we have it. What more can be said?

"And so, my dear friend, I believe it is time that we turn our attentions from the absurdities of this *something/nothing* dichotomy to the nature and beauty of *emptiness* instead. You see, I am neither *nothing* nor *something*, as you understand them. I am *emptiness*, neither a doughnut nor not a doughnut, for infinite things are *not doughnuts* and it is the *emptiness* of a doughnut that makes a doughnut – the doughnut in turn is the *emptiness* of its *emptiness*. And so it is with all *somethings* – they are the *emptiness* of their *emptiness*. So, too, even with *nothing*, which in turn is the *emptiness* of its *emptiness*."

Thus – in the back kitchen, on a high shelf – the doughnut, in embracing its *emptiness*, attained satori while awaiting the snack break of the second shift dishwasher. And the dishwasher, who had placed it there early in the day, reaching up found neither *something* nor *nothing* but only the *emptiness* of *emptiness* where a doughnut and a hole had once been.

Helen Morley's Finger
(In the Days of Steno Pools)

Prologue

Taoist philosopher Lieh Tzu believed that whatever is chanced upon by the spirit is the stuff of dreams, but that which is chanced upon by the body is the stuff of happenings and encounters. What neither spirit nor body can explain or understand are the comings and goings and transformations of the world of things.[1]

The owner of the delicatessen down the street was fascinated by the gloved index finger on Helen Morley's right hand. Saturdays when she did her shopping he would nibble her in the mirrors of mirrors up and down the aisles where she squeezed along from the bread to the bananas, thumped canned goods and watermelons (in season). No matter how firmly the rest of the gloved hand committed itself to a tomato's ripeness, a grape's state of juice, one glove finger stood rigid, ready like some wild animal sentinel to spring – as if possessed of the same rabbit fear that peered from her wet, gray eyes above the little peroxided mustache. Her narrow face was streamlined in a bun at the back of her head as though to offer less wind resistance in flight.

He never stopped her, partly from pity, partly from respect for her deceased father, a wealthy attorney. A strong, fierce man, her father had served as an officer in France in World War I and always wore at least one of his medals attached to his lapel.

"A real tiger he was...yessir! I remember once I'd took some kolbassa up to the apartment...she was at work and the old guy let me in hisself. My god, what a place! All that African stuff and heads on the walls, but real ones…and he'd shot 'em all hisself over there. Well, he seen how interested I was and he told me about each one of 'em and how he'd almost been et a hundred times by elephants and lions and giraffes. But the damndest thing, right there on the mantel, was this glass of stuff…looked like water…and a hand in it! Of course I knew he'd lost one…someplace in the first war. He said he'd been trapped in a tank or somethin' like that. He wasn't keen to talk about it and I didn't want to pry…but there it was, the old guy still had it starin' at 'im…damndest thing I ever seen…"

Her mother had passed on while Helen was quite small and she had been raised by the cook. Her father was too seldom home to assume much of this sort of task. When Helen was sixteen he fired the cook. Helen took her place.

That she might not waste her time when he wasn't there to be cared for, he sent her to a secretarial school. "Either a woman marries to raise a family and keep house, or she learns to feed herself. You've got a house and your own family to take care of, so there's no need for marriage, but when I'm gone you'll have to take care of yourself. This way you've got the best of both cakes of cheese, with no man around your neck who's a bum."

Halfway through the secretarial course she was in a car accident. He was driving and drunk – a pity, as he said, because otherwise she might have sued. Helen broke her right arm in two places and lost her index finger. At school she had to shift her finger pattern on the typewriter, but still graduated at the top of her class. The same automobile accident injured the reflex in her left foot so that as she walked its gentle flapping raised small puffs of dust in the summer, or snow in the winter.

She got a job in the secretarial pool of one of his clients' firms. After typing all day, she dusted the stuffed heads, vacuumed the rugs and prepared dinner. Before her father became bedridden, he took her check at the end of the month and gave her an allowance. Later, when constant care was necessary, the check went to the string of male nurses who wrestled the old 'tiger'.

Any secretary new to the pool was confounded by the phenomenon of will and skill in that the fastest and most accurate of the typists was missing the entire index finger of her right hand! And every newcomer was quickly forced to choose a side in the controversy about Helen Morley's gloves that lived in the coffee room.

To conceal her deformity, Helen wore gloves at all seasons to and from the pool. The sleeve of the missing digit was stuffed with wool fuzz. When she relaxed or closed her right hand, the sleeve pointed like an asparagus stalk at the passing day.

One school of thought, with Ruth Thompson leading, insisted the stuffed glove was an intolerable absurdity. "She's certainly no beauty, no one's arguing that, but why should she go out of her way to make herself ridiculous?" "And she's always catching it on things and in doors." "It just makes it worse – I've seen the way people stare at her on the street and in the stores."

The other school, larger by one, was led by Ruth's rival for section supervisor, Alice Crowder. Not so outspoken as Ruth, Alice brought a more subtle psychological insight to her point of view. "But that's it, the poor dear needs anything she can get to bolster her soggy ego." "If it helps let her do it." "That's no worse than bleaching her mustache."

Occasionally, through promotion or pregnancy, the balance shifted from one side to the other, but the change was never so solid that one of the leaders might feel secure enough to speak to Helen Morley directly about the glove. That other people noticed her was certainly true. Most of them assumed, like the owner of the delicatessen, that she had a severed tendon and so were not faced with the enlightened choices of the members of the pool.

Helen Morley's interest in the pool, for as long as those who worked there could remember, had never gone beyond typing at great speed what she was given to reproduce. She drank no coffee with the girls. She lunched alone. Rumor intimated that she was Mormon, though one of the girls claimed to have seen her "drinking coffee in Woolworth's one Saturday. She thinks she's fooling us."

She didn't drink coffee nor did she think herself better than the others. A childhood of stuffed animals' glass glances and the old man's pickled rages had early atrophied all self-assurance…and coffee and alcohol upset her stomach. Helen liked the delicatessen's "mild green tea…with the tang of distant adventure sealed in every bag at the factory."

The death of her father altered the substructure of Helen's world little. His "Goddammit woman, where's the you know what?" no longer disturbed her sleep, but the glazed animal stares that spied on her while he was alive now posted their observations to him beyond the grave, where someday he would confront her with all she had done or neglected to do in his absence. The raised trunk of the elephant still threatened obscenely to seize her when she dusted it, but she was more afraid not to dust. The tiger's promised roar reminded her of her father's flawless teeth arched in a grimace when something displeased him.

In the evenings the tall, thick-shaded floor lamps lighted smoky fires in the yellows and oranges of their eyes. On the high, dim ceiling antelope prongs fenced vast parallelograms around the elephant's tusked erection. Deer, intent on the marlin above the buffet, pointed their ears for the lion sounds of dripping saliva. When she turned the lamps off, the room was thick with their waiting. Even though she slept with the door to her bedroom locked, she could hear them whispering beyond the wall.

The apartment exuded the dark masculine scent of the hunt. It was as strong in the kitchen, where half-full bottles of expensive gins, whiskies, and brandies still thronged the cupboards, as in the bathroom, where three straight razors, two shaving mugs and a year's supply of shaving soap lived in the medicine chest. Only in her room was there a break in the pattern. The rug was a little brighter. The high ceiling was kept at a distance by a spiraling lace canopy over the bed. The smells from the bottles on the dressing table thinned the dense musk that came in under the door.

After his death she thought of subletting part of the enormous apartment, but was afraid of the heads…and besides…he would not approve. A guilty glance at the glass containing the hand on the mantel scattered such thoughts.

She had deliberated before the burial on whether the hand should be enclosed in the coffin. "We can attach it in the sleeve and with a little coloring it would appear as if it had never been severed," the mortician had assured her when she asked his advice. For sentimental reasons she hadn't included it. After all it had been a part of her father as a young man, before the world had superimposed its cares upon him. There was a picture next to the hand of the virile young officer in his high-collared uniform, his hair slicked back, the two hands folded in his lap. She liked to think that the hand in the glass – by some miracle – had never aged the way its companion had. The other was eroded with swollen veins flowing about arthritic mounds, its muscles helpless to lift it from the sheets. (Might almost the same miracle have happened to her finger...if it had been salvageable and salvaged?) Besides...those terrible heads couldn't really hurt her with the young officer's hand there...

The picture frame she covered with black ribbon, but the hand...black seemed inappropriate! Six months after the funeral, in desperate loneliness, she placed a little bud vase near the glass and kept a fresh red rose in it. Gradually the animals shed their terrors, as if the rose met their approval. They stopped whispering. Their eyes glazed. They slept.

Once when she returned later than usual from the office – several of the staff had been ill – as she stopped before the door to search for the key, the finger caught in the straps of her purse and she dropped everything in trying to disengage it. Coins rolled in all directions. She bent to retrieve them and heard the crash of breaking glass from the apartment! When she opened the door, the air smelled of alcohol.

The marble hearth was covered with glass fragments; both the bottle and the vase had fallen and broken. The hand and the rose lay together on the pile rug a few inches further away.

"My God, my God!" Her eyes raced about the room seeking an explanation, paused briefly at the elephant's head as though suspecting his trunk, but that was too far...he couldn't have...

She picked up the hand and laid it gently on her handkerchief on the table. This was the first time she had ever seen it out of the fluid or touched it. It was firm and slightly warm as though the fireplace had been burning.

She emptied what rubbing alcohol she could find into a fruit jar and then, without cleaning up the mess, rushed to the all-night drugstore on Second Avenue for another quart.

How could it have happened? An earth tremor? A passing subway train that she had missed in the excitement of finding her keys?

The next day she bought a new bud vase and two rose buds.

Three days before the end of January there was a light, dry snowfall. It had begun about noon and some of the staff had used the 'blizzard' as an excuse to leave early. At 4:30 Mrs. Calvin from Accounting brought in a stack of admonition letters on various overdue accounts. Because the accounts were all sizable and Mrs. Calvin wanted to be firm without antagonizing, each letter softened the sharp black of its numerals with the pastel of its individual tone. Each would have to be done separately. Mrs. Calvin retreated to Accounting. Two more women staff members vanished on the way to the supply room. By five, only Helen and two others remained to finish the stack.

It was seven before she left. An inch and a half of powder swirled underfoot – too dry to pack except where an underground source of warmth took the subzero chill off the ground and melted an ice flow across the sidewalk. There was no wind. The broken reflex in her foot cast a snow shadow several times larger than the shoe.

"I've got to get some mittens," she thought…then she could leave the gloves with their dilemma at home. She knew of the controversy, but avoided it as she avoided the animal eyes, avoided his half-full bottles of whiskey in the cupboards…though sometimes she thought of opening them and drowning all those heads in their contents! But…where would it stop? Wouldn't she drown too? Why didn't she want to drown? No! To think that way! She tried to visualize him sitting silent, solid at the table…or at least to recall the photo on the mantel…the young man's hand next to it. These visions almost always steadied her.

When she opened the door to the dark apartment, she heard a strange sound, like a great cat lightly padding across the blackness. She quickly turned on the light in the entryway and tried to peer into the living room. The room exposed in the door's trapezoid was vague and noncommittal. She switched on the floor lamp. The room was as she had left it, yet changed. She did not look at the heads…glanced at the photo to steady her nerves…saw the lid was off the fruit jar and drops of alcohol were scattered near the glass. The hand didn't appear to have been disturbed…had someone been in the room…opened the glass?

As she coordinated her various sense impressions with possible explanations, a terrible feeling of another presence in the room pressed against the back of her neck. Should she scream…run out in the hall? She edged back to the door, opened it, and backed into the rows of apartments. They assured her enough that she could examine the lock on the door. There was no evidence it had been forced, no scratches on the key plate or wood frame.

Down the hall a door opened and a couple came out. They stared at her, then walked toward the elevator. The man pressed the button. "The Wilsons"…she recognized them and quickly limped back into her own entryway. She knew they were watching her. She closed the door.

Most of the people on the landing she knew from the elevator, but, like her father, she avoided any closer acquaintance. A cold formality separated all the entries from one another. The inhabitants had their own interests and outside friends.

The sight of the Wilsons had sobered her enough that she could return to the living room. The apartment door had not been pried…was there no disturbance except on the mantel? She turned on the lights in the other rooms. No one. The twenty dollar bill in the corner of her mirror was still there. She put the lid on the jar and wiped up the alcohol stains where the liquid had now dried.

In the kitchen she warmed a TV dinner. She didn't want to sit in the living room with the heads…it was almost as if they had been awakened again. After supper she went to her room to read in bed. She wouldn't look at the ceiling, even in her own room, and was glad that the canopy was there between the white sheets and the vault.

For several days afterward, she couldn't approach the outer door without her fear returning. She was anxious in all the rooms of the apartment except her own and she began to take her supper there to eat on the dressing table. She moved the photo from the mantel to the table in the living room that like a talisman it might restore the apartment to normal.

Beyond her closed door at night she occasionally heard the animals whispering again. Sometimes she awoke in the dark with a start…had she sensed some peculiar sound in her sleep? She listened intently till the clock fractured the darkness with its alarming wail.

Finally she moved the photo and the fruit jar into her room onto the dressing table. For several nights she slept soundly.

The temperature outside dropped steadily. The only pauses in the cold came in mid-February in short bursts of moist air and heavy snow. Many of the women were absent with the flu. Her health held…nothing more serious than an occasional headache. Toward the end of February, however, she developed a harsh cough and a mild fever. By that time the situation in the pool was critical. Almost half the staff was gone. She did not feel she could stay away from work even a single day.

In the middle of one particularly taxing afternoon, plagued by a splitting headache and mild nausea, she left her typewriter to join the others for coffee…certain that she would not make it through the afternoon without some sort of drastic assistance…perhaps coffee…

The fact that most of the absent women were from the other side gave Ruth courage and she began a conversation that moved fleetingly from surprise that Helen did drink coffee after all, to a comment about how pale she was, to pleasant agreement with the fact that she was now wearing mittens, to the question of whether or not she knew how ridiculous the stuffed glove had made her look – it hadn't fooled anybody.

Helen mumbled something and took the paper cup to her desk – a serious breach of one of the pool's rules. No one protested.

At home that night she didn't bother to heat a TV dinner, but went straight to her room, took two aspirin and went to bed.

About midnight she was suddenly awakened! Something had happened in the room! As she lay still, holding her heart back, trying to recall what she might have heard on the periphery of sleep…she noticed a dripping sound coming from the dressing table. She switched on the light above her head and got up. The jar lay on its side, the lid off, alcohol dribbled onto the dressing bench. The hand lay on the floor.

There wasn't anyone else in the room, the door was still locked …she even looked in the closet and glanced under the bed.

She stopped to pick up the hand. The fall had spread the fingers and in order to return it to the glass she had to force them back into place. As she pressed them together she found them as warm and plastic as her own…a shudder flowed up her arm. She began to cry in convulsing gasps. She half fell, half sat on the edge of the bed, unaware that she still clutched the hand until, several minutes later, a firm pressure on her own fingers startled her!

The preserved tendons in the hand, reacting to the nervous tension of her grip, must have closed the fingers about her own. The clasp was at once sobering and comforting, almost tender, in a way the old man had certainly never been. For a moment she was overwhelmed by her loneliness. Still holding the hand that firmly gripped around her own, she walked over to the photograph. The young man there in his uniform was straight and sober, but the eyes were kindly. The old man's eyes had been bloodshot and inflamed from alcohol and too many trips to the sun.

She returned the hand to the glass, though the reflexes had continued to resist her attempts to disengage the fingers. After she had cleaned as much of the alcohol as she could from the rug, she lay awake for a long time trying to make sense of all that crowded in on her splitting head. The animals fortunately were not whispering. The apartment was quiet.

When she finally slept, the young soldier with the high collar and kindly eyes gently opened her door and led her by the hand through the wall and out into a grassy valley where animals of indistinct sorts and sizes roamed the ridges. The two of them sat down on a small grassy knoll. He was pointing at something in the distance…she couldn't quite understand what he was saying…the voice that she knew was that of a fractious old man…and this was another's. As she strained to see what he intended, she noticed that on the rim before them the animals had stopped moving aimlessly and had begun descending the slopes…sideways…as though to conceal their intent. Even at that distance, even before she could clearly distinguish their forms, she could see the hard yellow-orange eyes. He seemed oblivious to their movements. When she tried to speak, she couldn't.

She attempted to rise, but her legs were lost in the grass…he was still pointing into the distance. The pressure of his hand on hers began to increase, timed it seemed to the approach of the animals... did he see them, then? The greater the hurt the closer they came...so close she could now hear them breathing, their paws sliding through the grass...and still he sat there!

The cold shock of her own cooling sweat awakened her. The cover had slipped from the bed. The first signs of the sun fired the canopy's lace. As she turned to retrieve the blanket she rolled onto something hard in bed. Raising herself on her elbow she found the hand...its fingers twisted into her gown. She recoiled so violently that it rolled onto the floor with a gentle thump. She must have fetched it in her sleep...the overturned jar lay on the rug near the bench.

For the third time she picked it up. It was warm from her body heat and soft to the touch, the fingers as pliable as though on a living hand.

She straightened the jar and started to place the hand into it. Suddenly the gentle pressure of the dream was back. She attempted to disengage the fingers with her left hand, but the pressure increased at once and began to hurt! The warmed tendons held her fast. It was impossible to turn it loose. The pressure relaxed when she relaxed, but was there immediately if she tried to put the hand into the bottle.

She could see the animals along the walls. She tripped over the bench and fell against the dressing table, knocking the jar to the floor. A cream container rolled off after it and shattered it. In her fall, the hand had relaxed its grip, but she hadn't noticed. She knelt on the floor for several minutes before she realized the hand was lying quietly on the dressing table. How had it gotten there?

The grandfather clock in the living room began striking nine o'clock. Years of habit took over motor control from her groping mind and carried her into the bathroom, dressed her and walked her out the door. Even the idea of lateness, her first time in ten years, did not reach a conscious plane until she was already on the bus and surrounded by women with small children, instead of gray office workers.

Mrs. Calvin stopped by her desk to collect some forms that afternoon that she had left there earlier in the day...they were still unprocessed..."Are you ill?"...concerned but not unkindly.

Mrs. Calvin respected her, "…one of the staff you can always count on. Of course she has her peculiarities. I've never seen anyone quite so…so…yes…so…withdrawn…yes, withdrawn…sort of dried up, you know, like a prune."

"Go home, dear, and go to bed. It must be the flu. I'll get someone else to take care of these."

She was not only having hallucinations, she had been late for work…and now…what had happened? Where had she been all day? She couldn't neglect her work. There wasn't anything else! By four it was obvious she couldn't sit at her desk any longer. Errors completely corroded whatever she tried to do.

What awaited her at home? She couldn't clearly recall the events of the previous night. She didn't want to. At the drugstore she purchased another quart of alcohol and bought an attractive candy jar with sealing lid. At the apartment, she paused before the door and listened. There were only the normal hall noises.

In the apartment, the evening's half-light coated everything with a thick dusk. She took her hat off and went into the kitchen, the brightest room when the light was on, and made a pot of strong tea. After she had drunk two cups she took her coat off and laid it over a chair, then went into the living room.

The sun had set and the room was quickly darkening. She did not turn the lights on. She washed her face in the bathroom before going into her room. In the bedroom, because it had a south window, there was more light and she could make out the form of the tumbled bed through the lace curtain. She hesitated for several minutes in the doorway, staring at the receding light on the window drape. She did not look in the direction of the dressing table.

When it became too dark to see, she switched on the ceiling light…blinked in its brightness…quickly and brusquely walked to the dressing table. The hand lay exactly as she had left it. Cold and stiff now. She picked it up with her handkerchief and hastened with it to the kitchen. The increasing warmth went through the cloth and the stiff fingers began to relax.

She set it on the sink drain and unpacked the candy glass. From the cupboard she fetched what was left of the other bottle of rubbing alcohol. Out of the corner of her eye she thought she saw a finger move.

She grabbed the half-empty bottle from among the whiskies that flanked it and returned to the sink. The lid slipped out of her nervous fingers and clattered into the basin. The sound of metal on metal startled her and she spilled some of the contents onto her hand. It was cold. A thin, antiseptic smell wrinkled her nose.

She glanced at the lid resting on the drain, bent slightly to retrieve it. Her fingers and thumb, however, instead of seizing the lid closed on the knob of the drain. She lifted the cover out and looked at its holes as though trying to remember what the strainer was for.

From the strainer to the candy glass…her eyes skimmed over the white form on the counter…had it moved? She dropped the strainer onto the drainboard and seized the hand. Before her nerves had time to register its texture, she stuffed it stump first into the basin's cavity and turned on the disposal and the hot water…shoved the fingers down with the dish brush. There was a dull edge to the sound for a moment as the grinders caught the bones, then the water drained the sounds off…she poured the rubbing alcohol into the sink, emptied the new bottle after it. She went to the cupboard and seized the first two bottles…dumped one of them in, started to empty the second but changed her mind and placed the neck to her lips, coughed, spit, and pulled another mouthful in and down.

The kitchen smelled of good bourbon. Steam covered the window above the sink. She threw the empty bottle into the basin where it broke, sending splinters into and around the grinding hole. A speck of blood appeared on her forehead. She took her coat from the chair, the mittens from its pocket and pushed them into the disposal. From the utility drawer she removed a screwdriver and ran into the living room. Perching on one chair then another, she began prying the eyes out of the heads. Whenever she had a handful she dropped them down the hole, which belched a gritty response. After she had the elephant's eyes, she fetched a hammer and shattered his tusks. The head hung askew, the trunk was twisted…

As she pushed the fragments of trunk into the steaming mouth, she remembered the photo in the bedroom. When she tilted the frame to remove the picture, she suddenly noticed the plate behind the glass was blank…

Metamorphosis

Prologue

The Buddhist term *anatta* means *no-self.* This is not to deny that we as individuals have feelings, sensations, thoughts and memories, bodies, predispositions. However, there is no 'owner' of these feelings, sensations, thoughts, memories, and predispositions apart from these transitory states. Thus, the Buddhist *Visuddhi-magga*[1] tells us that *misery* certainly exists, but there is *no* miserable *owner* of this misery, just as there is *action* too, but no *actor.*

The Jaina Sutras in turn analyze the origins and types of life forms we encounter:

> "...those who are produced 1. From eggs (birds, etc.), 2. From a fetus (as elephants, etc.), 3. From a fetus with an enveloping membrane (as cows, buffaloes, etc.), 4. From fluids (as worms, etc.), 5. From sweat (as bugs, lice, etc.), 6. By coagulation (as locusts, ants, etc.), 7. From sprouts (as butterflies, wagtails, etc.), 8. By generation (men, gods, hell-beings). This is called the Samsara for the slow, for the ignorant. Having well considered it, having well looked at it, I say thus: all beings, those with two, three, four senses, plants, those with five senses, and the rest of creation, (experience) individual pleasure or displeasure, pain, great terror and unhappiness. Beings are filled with alarm from all directions and in all directions."[2]

Monday afternoon fifty gallons of liquid insecticide arrive. Tuesday morning they are diluted with one hundred and fifty gallons of water from the Experimental Farm's artesian well, which is forty-five feet deep and slightly alkaline. Wednesday three acres of tomato plants are sprayed. The mixture is toxic enough for twenty even though the tomato hornworm are running from six to ten per plant. The heavy concentrate is a measure of the Director's dislike. The fleshy, green worms with their streaked and dotted yellow slashes and protruding, harmless horns nauseate the Director. Thursday morning the ground is laced with browning bits of green worm. The few leaves on the plants, burned by the concentrate, are curled.

In the left corner of the field the sun holds steady on a pool of blue insecticide in which a hard-shelled, spindle-shaped hornworm cocoon floats. The heat gradually grounds the cocoon as the sun sucks the last vapors from the earth around it. Thursday evening a light rain falls. The drops knock the spindle about, thoroughly chilling it.

Friday morning, sometime between midnight and 5:50 when the sun first breaks the eastern horizon, the imprisoned form goes into its final stage and the cocoon begins to crack. No hawk moth emerges. Instead of antennae the shape that pulls itself out of the shell has eyes. Where wings should be there are arms and hands. There are two legs instead of six. They terminate in feet and toes.

The long sucking proboscis is stunted and punctuated with two nostrils, below which a toothy mouth snaps and gasps at the air. Its nose itches. The figure scratches it with one hand – discovering in the gesture its fingers. It waves its arms. They slice the air but it cannot fly.

The two legs are unstable. It falls several times before learning to place one foot before the other and shift the weight of the upright body accordingly.

After the eyes become conditioned to squinting at the rising sun, the figure becomes more self-assured, walks forward a few steps and stumbles over a swollen hornworm. It kicks the leathery hide with its foot. The worm breaks. Cool fluid dribbles across bare toes. With a twig it enlarges the hole through which the collapsing body drains. The sides shrivel together until only the horn remains erect on the flabby carcass. The wreck is funny. The figure laughs. The sun scorches. To the left a worm explodes in the heat with the dull snap of a rubber band on slate. The figure crawls into the leafless branches to avoid the direct rays, but finds scant shade and is able to protect itself only by pressing its body close to the hard, scaly stalks. As the sun nears noon, the popping of rubber bands marks the progress of the day at the rate of several a minute. These decline in the afternoon. A single last worm explodes a half hour after the sun disappears.

As the evening earth cools, the screeching of night birds supplants the sounds of bursting worms. Leaving the branches, the figure returns to the carcass where the horn still holds itself in a proud, brittle erection. The fluid has dried and the residue reeks of rotten tomatoes. The skin has crusted. The wrecks of thousands of dirigible worms are littered about...deflated and stiff-horned, surrounded by armies of naked vines. Where worms once fed on the succulent leaves, dry skeletons crackle and rasp. Crickets cough. The figure shivers, beats its hands on its body till they are warm again. It begins to run. Halfway across the field there are no cricket noises. It discovers a gently panting mound of night bird, beak split wide and held askew by its twisted tongue. The bird's large, sharp eyes are half-sheathed in whitish lids over which the live creature stares desperately. The wing-tip feathers mark a rustling dance against the hard ground...then stop. The tongue thrusts quickly in and out, finally locks in the out position. The mound is still.

The figure strokes the warm feathers. They are soft and soothe its hand. It buries its head in the downy underside where the fuzz tickles its ears. It sneezes and realizes it is hungry.

At the edge of the field it finds a heavy clover growth and tries to eat the bitter leaves. Then it crosses under a fence and skirts along the edge of a road. There it trips over a large strawberry, the remnant of an earlier experiment. The berry smells good. The figure devours it, sets off in search of another. Suddenly a truck grinds by, thrusting into the night with jerky lights, and trembling the earth. Frightened, the figure flees back into the dense clover to cower under a rain-pocked clod of earth.

Overhead the stars prophesy the moon. Their cries are small and fragile against the nothingness of the hollow sky. Once more the figure ventures in the direction of the strawberry, but falls in the lightless clover jungle. Something breaks its fall. It cannot rise. Ropes tense around its hands and feet, spread its twitching fingers...give when it strains against them, gently tighten again when it tires...like a starfish cajoling a clam, lightly pulling with its suckers until the stronger prey is exhausted and the shell opens easily, permitting the star to project its tender stomach inside.

The moon at last fractures the edge of the night, slivering into the forest in octagonal clover circles. Out from the splintered shadow the voices of the night begin to croak and sing. The stomach of the darkness testily prances on eight arched velvet legs in the shattered light.

The threads tense into steel strings. The heartbeat of their captive vibrates across the net in the moonlight like ripples upon the surface of a pond disturbed by small fish nosing for air. Guided by the moon and the rippling strings, the night delivers its caresses. Retreats. Returns. Caresses again. Retreats. The struggle with the web is over. The ripple continues where the heart, too secure to be probed, keeps the blood flowing and the body alive. The eyes are wide. Rolling back at the moon until the lids deck the dilated pupils. Only the white slips through.

The figure is embraced by two downy legs and eased toward the dark funnel near the center of the net. Here the air is warm. In the nest of the night the legs position the figure as though for some mystic rite. The moon curves in its course to peer for a moment into the den where already snuggled against the naked breast of the guest are two large, white eggs.

Christians and Buddhists at Winter Solstice

Prologue

The lion as the king of beasts is the great meat eater and predator. The Indian Panchatantra makes it clear that even should there be no meat, the lion still will not graze the grass.[1] To which insight the Buddhist adds in the *Digha Nikaya*:

> "...once long ago the lion, king of beasts, thought: 'Suppose I were to make my lair near a certain jungle. Then I could emerge in the evening, yawn, survey the four quarters, roar my lion's roar three times, and then make for the cattle-pasture. I could then pick out the very best of the herd for my kill and, having had a good feast of tender meat, return to my lair.' And he did accordingly."[2]

In the scriptures of the Hebrews and Christians we find innumerable reminders of the lion's 'meat lust' and its dreadful implications for human beings both spiritually and physically, for as Jesus said: "Blessed is the lion which a man eats so that the lion becomes a man. But cursed is the man whom a lion eats so that the man becomes a lion!"[3] But perhaps most terrible of all in the sacred texts is the danger that Satan as the 'lion spirit' poses for all true believers:

> "Save me from all them that pursue me, and deliver me, lest they tear my soul like a lion, rending it in pieces, while there is none to deliver."
> (*Psalms* 7:1-2)
> "Be sober, be watchful: your adversary the devil, as a roaring lion, walketh about, seeking whom he may devour."
>
> (*I Peter* 5:8)

"And he that overcometh, and he that keepeth my
works unto the end, to him will I give authority over
the nations; and he shall rule them with a rod of iron,
as the vessels of the potter are broken to shivers..."
                                        (*Revelations* 2:26-7)
"He that overcometh shall inherit these things; and
I will be his God, and he shall be my son. But for
the fearful, and unbelieving, and abominable, and
murderers, and fornicators, and sorcerers, and
idolaters, and all liars, their part shall be in the lake
that burneth with fire and brimstone..."
                                        (*Revelations* 21:7-8)

Historians are painters, and like painters they select not
only their subjects, but also their colors and brushes. They
determine the width of their strokes, their shapes, thickness,
and numbers. As a result, the finished product, the text or painting,
is an autobiographical product drawn from its creator's aesthetic
feelings, assumptions, and choices. Most historical 'paintings'
are done with very broad strokes. One historian colors with
revolutions and wars, another with economic cycles, a third with
population migrations, a fourth with ideologies. There are a few
'pointillists', but most of these too are after a total effect and not
the separate points with which they create their images and tales.
However, life is not broad strokes, and history as it appears in the
books and newspapers never happens.

The real are the moments, the particular situations, and these
in infinite number. It is these immediate happenings that are the
sources of the most complex historical events just as a single pebble
thrown upon a pond surface becomes the source of ever expanding
and crisscrossing rings. Sometimes these moments are positive as in
the case of the wick Mrs. O'Leary was using in her lantern when she
milked her cow. Without this wick, no lantern light, no Chicago fire.
Sometimes they are negative like the non-breaking of a single
oarsman's oar, which might then have sent Washington's party
in circles instead of across the Delaware. Sometimes it is a mix of

both. For example, Benvenuto Cellini, the great Italian Renaissance goldsmith, felt that it was only someone's parsimony that spared his life in the prison where he was to be dispatched instead of compensated for works he had delivered. Cellini was certain he would have perished had he been given the prescribed ground diamond instead of ground glass, which subsequently passed through his system.

The following true story is a tale of one such brief event as it registered in the awareness of a single young man at a moment critical to the development of Christianity. To revisit the story, we must return to the reign of Diocletian (CE 285-307), the last pagan emperor to securely rule a unified Roman empire.

By the second century CE, the glory that was Rome had spread from the coasts of Asia Minor to North Africa, through southern Europe and Spain to the British Isles. With the power and idea of 'Rome', spread also its fashions in dress, food, social behavior, and even entertainment. For example, it was one of the prestigious marks of the time for a community to have its version of the great Colosseum, no matter how scaled down or modified – an arena where gladiatorial combats and other sporting events could be held, a center for the general population where one might watch wild animals tear each other to pieces or, on special days, shred human beings. There one might have seen one of Menander's or Aristophanes' comedies or one of Seneca's tragedies. When nothing else was available, there were races and oratory contests.

By the end of the third century, however, the empire was disintegrating. After the death of Emperor Caracalla in 217, each of the next sixteen emperors was assassinated – many of them reigning less than two years. Conflicts between rulers, 'would-be rulers', and their descendants were common. Invasions of migrating tribes from

Northern and Eastern Europe threatened to break through the Roman defenses and perhaps destroy Rome itself. The silver coinage had been reduced to bronze, plated with a thin silver coating. Most trade and commerce relied on barter. Temples and palaces, with the exception of those of the corrupt imperial tax collectors, were the victims of disrepair and decay.

The quality of entertainment in the arenas had radically deteriorated as well, offering low budget grade B circuses and part-time, middle-aged gladiators listlessly hacking away at one another's paunches. Local theatre groups, which were often only semiliterate and reciting texts badly, replaced the travelling companies sent out from the great cities. Even when slurred, a drunken rendition of Menander's "Counterfeit Baby" seemed appropriate to the time:

> "That man, O Parmenon, I count most fortunate
> Who quickly whence he came returns.
> While he that tarries longer, worn, his money gone,
> Grows old and wretched and forever knows some lack.
> A vagrant he, the sport of enemies and plots.
> Gaining no easy death the transient guest returns."[4]

Often the high point of festivities dedicated to one of the gods might be little more than rounds of oratorical declamations by local politicians followed by a 'catch the greased slave' contest. Few towns could afford real wild animals for their wild animal bouts and large dogs were often painted with leopard spots or had their tails dressed and their necks ringed with rabbit fur to make them look like lions. Occasionally a cat would be tossed into such a contest in order to lend a certain amount of authenticity. Some of the more primitive German communities in the north trained herds of small badger dogs to dog-pile thieves and tax evaders to death before cheering and desperate crowds.

Such was the situation when Diocletian succeeded to the imperial title in 284. The son of a Dalmatian slave, he had risen through the internal power struggles that characterized the decaying empire. Diocletian was a capable general and a superb administrator who realized that if Rome was to survive, order and ruthless discipline had to be restored in an administrative system that would centralize all power under the control of a single ruler and his immediate deputies, whose allegiance could be assured if their sons were attached to his retinue, where they might both learn the ways of administration and at the same time serve as hostages for their fathers' performances. One of the most important examples of this system was the assignment of Constantine, the son of General Constantius I Chlorus, to Diocletian's court.

Diocletian also realized that to renew and revitalize the state, each community had to be renewed and revitalized. This he sought to achieve by returning silver to the coins, rebuilding crumbling roads, strengthening the borders, repairing older temples, and dedicating new ones. He also clearly understood that the empire was spiritually united by the temple ritual in each community and the worship of the gods, including the deified emperors. This policy brought him into conflict with a growing Christian minority throughout the empire, a minority that was not necessarily pacifistic, but one that was reluctant to worship outside its own temples or to participate in state religious festivals. Thus it was Diocletian, that last great pagan emperor of a unified empire, who also decreed the last great pagan purging of Christians from the army and government service, for he viewed them as a threat to the state's stability and well-being.

As Diocletian traveled from province to province, local religious and sports festivals celebrated his arrival. If they could be located in time, bears would be pitted against dogs or spear-armed warriors. If there were prisoners of war, robbers, military deserters, members of official families that had fallen from favor, obstinate Christians or Jews, these could be tossed to whatever assault species was available.

And so it came to pass that on the eve of the winter solstice in 300, Diocletian and his court found themselves in Aquileia. The city had been preparing for weeks for a combined celebration of the Emperor's arrival and the birth of Mithra at the winter solstice. The crumbling arena had been repaired, the marble replaced in the imperial box. Aquileia like all cities at the end of the third century was in narrowed financial straits – though as a port city it had advantages over cities inland for it had access to sea trade where among other goods, it could from time to time also secure wild beasts for its public events. Of course the wild beast market had also been affected by the general decline in the empire. The securing of a first-rate lion, leopard, bear, or wolf was both difficult and prohibitively expensive. What was available went to Rome or Byzantium or Spalatum (Diocletian's palace).

Fortunately, however, two days before the Emperor's scheduled arrival a wild beast order placed early in the summer arrived – an African lion. What the council did not realize until too late was that the official responsible for placing the order had spent much of the money on the renovation of his own summer palace in Cibalae. The resulting shortage of funds was reflected in the quality of lion that had been secured. What arrived was a rather elderly and worn beast, many of whose teeth were missing, and whose hide was spotted with patches of bare skin. The mane was matted and dirty and mostly missing on one side. Nonetheless, it was a lion and certainly a vast improvement over a Dalmatian with rabbit fur, which the Emperor might well have taken as a personal insult. The official had mysteriously disappeared shortly before the lion arrived and was not to be located.

The question now was who could or should be fed to the lion for the Emperor's edification. There were three pickpockets, two petty thieves, and four army deserters in the city's prison. However, none of these were deemed appropriate to the occasion where the king of beasts, before the king of men, on the auspicious day of the birth of the king of gods, would tear someone to shreds. Then one of those little miracles occurred that have always buoyed the beliefs of the believing and confounded the doubt of the doubting. A young man was found in the public square of Aquileia knocking the genitalia off the assembled stone gods and deified emperors there. He was apprehended just as he had finished with the great statue of Augustus and was heading for the imposing challenge offered by a local image of the Greek god Priapus, who predated the Roman conquest and who enjoyed especial worship by the city fathers.

The prefect thanked whatever gods were observing the young man's assault for answering his prayer, though he did muse at the interesting manner in which that prayer had been answered. Perhaps it was no less than Priapus himself who had warned the soldiers before his own member could be removed. Even greater and more miraculous was the prefect's wonder when he discovered upon questioning the young vandal, that he was a Christian and felt it his inspired duty to deface the gods – so to speak. The young man was chained to the wall in the same chamber in the arena's holding area in which the lion was confined in a cage. The prefect's assumption was that by locking them up together, though clearly separated, the lion's appetite would be whetted and the young rogue's insolence would in turn be tenderized by terror.

At first the young man's eyes could see nothing in the dark. It was clear, from the heavy breathing and the sour smell, that there was another living presence in the room…a large human being, or even perhaps an animal. It was only with the first morning light coming through the air hole at the east end of the chamber that he was able to recognize the other occupant, who was still sleeping.

When he distinguished the beast clearly, the young man sank to his knees and, with arms upraised, began to address the ceiling: "O blessed Lactantius! O merciful saints! O glorious Peter and Paul! O joy, o happiness, o rapture unbounded! My prayer is answered, a lion! A terrible, great, monstrous, blood-drooling beast with rending claws! A glorious death before the heathen emperor! O angels, you have heard my prayers and have seen fit at last to bless me with Christian martyrdom! I hear the doors of paradise beginning to swing wide! Soon the beast's jaws will crush my poor lifeless body and you will fetch my soul and confound the heathens! Then we shall return on horses of fire and with rods of iron smite them and impale them on our flaming swords!"

Then, noticing the lion had been awakened by his thanksgiving prayer, he half-addressed the beast. "But the question is what posture should I be holding when they turn you loose to shred my earthly body? How shall I go? Which position would be best? Should I kneel and pray with folded hands and eyes uplifted? Hmmm…the beast might seize my head first and I don't know whether I could still be holding my hands in prayer, especially if he knocks me over or drags me around by the neck. No, it might be better if I'm standing, hands upraised and eyes heaven bent. This would be especially effective if he only gnaws one leg at a time. Standing on one foot would be difficult of course, but maybe a sunbeam will fall on my uplifted face while the monster chews on the bloody stump. This would make a lasting impression on the spectators who will be trembling and the angels who will be watching my courageous martyring. Perhaps I should put my left hand on my breast where my heart, pure as driven snow, is beating its last…and extend my right hand with three fingers raised to bless my destroyer even in this terrible hour? That would certainly move the heathen crowd!

"Perhaps an angel will descend to collect my scattered remains and maybe even pull an arm or leg from the monster's jaws…better yet, remove my hand, still blessing my foe, from between his incisors…while at the same time a demon emerges from an opening in the ground and drags the son of Satan off to the eternal fires of hell! That would scare the unbelievers and heathens and give them something to think about. I can just hear the bloodthirsty roar of the beast transformed into a mousey squeak when he realizes the end he has brought upon himself by attacking one so pure and guiltless!

"Maybe a beatific smile of forgiveness even while the monster tears my forgiving hands off and my lifeblood spurts onto the coarse ground where later lilies will bloom. I wonder if I could pat his head gently, or kiss his terrible maw, a kiss of sorrow and forgiveness even as he tears my lips off. No…probably it would be best simply to stand arms outstretched waiting for the blessed angels to carry my martyred soul heavenward…"

A soft, throaty voice from the cage quietly interrupted this monologue to martyrdom. "I don't do Christians you know…in fact I don't do meat at all anymore."

The young man was so startled by this pronouncement – its content, not its possibility – that his leg chain rattled on the stone floor. "What? You're jesting! That's not true…that's nonsense. Everybody knows lions eat Christians. God made lions to eat Christians. That's why he gave them powerful claws, long teeth in cruel jaws, burning eyes…"

"My eyes do burn from time to time, that's true, but it's mostly from too much sun. That's why I have been enjoying the cool dark in here. And as for my teeth, some are slightly longish, but that's only on one side. I broke the others cracking nuts. And the ones that are left are most of them worn from eating roots and greens that always seem to have sand in them. Whether some lions may eat Christians I cannot say. I had friends and family a long time ago who did hunt gazelles and wildebeests and, on occasion, a human being. However, whether these were Christian or not I don't know – the men they ate were mostly black and I'm not sure what color Christians are. But as to who was made to eat whom…that seems to me a matter of belief and best left to village medicine men. In my case, I can assure you, I don't do Christians in particular, nor meat in general."

"But…that's unnatural! You're lying! You're trying to trick me! You want to lull me with a sense of security so that I won't show you up for what you are tomorrow out there in the arena…a monster, a brutal demon, a killing, butchering scourge rending my liver and rooting and snarling through my intestines, stuffing my still-throbbing heart into your cavernous maw…all the while writhing and gnashing your teeth and suffering horribly in the presence of my beatific and forgiving smile, incensed into madness in the presence of my hands clasped in prayer…and keenly aware that Beelzebub will fetch you once your terrible work is done, dragging you into hell fire by the tail! Admit it – even at this moment you cannot check the terrible flow of lustful slobber that drools from your mighty jaws and collects in puddles at your feet!"

"In a sense, you're right about the puddles part. Over the years I seem to have developed a weak kidney and lost a lot of control over my bladder. But that I expect is all part of growing older, and I do try to take it gracefully. I'm sorry if it offends you, but they haven't let me out of this cage for a while and it can't be helped."

At this point, the leg chain chattered violently against the floor as panic overwhelmed the man. "But you've got to rend and shred and tear and devour me! Everything depends upon it. My whole life, my martyrdom, my instant passage into the presence of Jesus and the blessed saints and angels in paradise. You have to maul me, squirt my blood around the arena. I've tried everywhere to be martyred. I insulted the gladiators in their locker rooms in Rome, only to be hooted out as too trivial and unworthy of their carving skills. In Verona, I was thrown with several others, mostly heathen Carthaginians and one Egyptian, into the pit with wolves who ate all the others and then lay down to sleep off their feeding frenzy without even glancing in my direction. Ever since, I've been looking for a lion who could martyr me in an appropriate fashion. This is my last chance. You must rend and rip me to bloody shreds. I will put in a good word for you, tell the blessed angels to keep the fires on low, plead with them that you were ignorant of the consequences of your actions…maybe even try to visit you in hell…but please, please, crush me in your great jaws, scatter my entrails around the arena, trying, of course, to let me hold my prayer pose as long as possible."

"Certainly I am a lion. That I have never denied. That was how I was born along with one brother and two sisters. In my youth, I thought there was no animal in the world that could compare to a lion. All the world feared and trembled before the lion, who could strike terror even into the elephant and her calf. No animal could plot and scheme like a pair of stalking lions!

"Ah, my friend. If we had met in my youth, things might have been otherwise. As a young lion ranging the great grasslands, I gloried in the hunt, the taste of raw meat burning in my nostrils when I tracked my prey. Occasionally I would trap a hunter who had been misled by his own cleverness into thinking he could trap me. I must confess, though, that I didn't care much for human flesh – too strong, an off taste, unpleasant even when a fresh kill. But even when I was very hungry I never took women or children, and to the best of my knowledge never ate a Christian, although I had a cousin who claimed he had eaten one of your kind, a whitish sort of priest or bishop or something. He said it gave him terrible gas pains.

"However, for all their strength, even lions are at the mercy of drought and fleeing game. During one of those scorching times that sweep across the grasslands and drive the zebra and gazelle and antelope away, my hunger forced me too into the rugged, low rock hills at the edge of the plain, where I hoped I might find some small creature sheltering in the brush.

"Wandering among the rocks there, I came upon an emaciated old man squatting on the ground chanting. I realized he wouldn't be much of a meal. In fact trying to chew up his bony carcass would probably take more energy than it would produce. But my stomach snarled that he was better than nothing at all. He didn't seem to have seen or smelled me yet. Staying downwind, I was preparing to clear the distance between us in one great leap, when he turned and stared at me crouching there! He didn't seem terrified or even surprised. You can imagine my astonishment! Prey usually screams and whines a lot – human or animal – but this one seemed totally indifferent. At first I thought it was a spasm or paralysis – which tends to make the meat tough.

"Then he twisted and thrust his foot in my direction, saying, 'Here start with this – it's as tender as it's going to get. No need to waste your energy on leaps – I'm not going anyplace. I'm not going to be much of a meal, but if you scrunch all the bones when you're done and get the marrow it will tide you over till something better comes along.'

"For a moment I was quite confused…firstly that he didn't try to escape and secondly that he was talking to me and I could understand him. This is an ability I've had ever since. When I came to my senses again, I roared a great roar, as if to drive off a bad dream full of crocodiles, and charged him, striking him with my paw. It wasn't a powerful blow, but he was little more than a skeleton and it knocked him over onto his back. Even then he didn't struggle, didn't even seem to care, and went right on talking with me as though nothing had happened except that he was doing a lot of gasping for breath."

"When he was able to speak again he said, 'So, you're a lion, a poor muscle-bound mound of lion meat. I've been waiting for you or someone like you, a leopard perhaps, to put an end to this pile of skin and bones. You're certainly welcome to whatever you find digestible. Of course eating me or any other creature won't end your hunger. It will only make more hunger possible just as any meal is created by all the meals that preceded it. You're the king of beasts, but the real king of the king of beasts is belly, and belly sitting on his hunger throne whips the poor old king of beasts with his desire for meat.'

"I didn't understand all of what he was saying and decided he was fooling me, trying to trick me out of devouring him…like some of the tricks animals pull, playing dead or rolling up in thorny balls. He seemed able to read my thoughts and pushing my paw off his chest and sitting up he said, 'You don't believe me, you're not satiated yet with hunger, you're still a lion, good – so be it. Here, get started!' and with that he pushed one foot right up under my nose. I call it a foot. It was more like a bird's claw, all covered with dirt and calluses and blisters and smelling like a jackal cache that had been dead for a thousand years. 'Come on, take a bite. It's as good a place as any to begin to give old belly his due and there's another when this one's done.'

"Well, my gut decided I had dallied enough and it gave my jaws and paws the start command. Eating his bony old carcass was like eating tree branches, and there wasn't even enough juice left in him to wash his scrawny foot down when it stuck sidewise in my throat.

"My hunger let up, but the worst of it was I kept imagining him chatting away in my gut. At first I thought it was gas, but it just never passed and after a while I started thinking over what he had said about the king of the king of beasts being belly sitting on a hunger throne whipping me with meat lust. That's when I started to talk back to belly. Tell it to shut up. There wouldn't be any meat for a while. Of course old belly didn't like that and he kicked up a fierce storm in there, screaming meat and more meat constantly. Then he started to devour me from the inside out, eating my flesh and drinking my blood so that I could hardly move. Even had I wanted to I couldn't have caught a mouse or a grasshopper. When I couldn't stand it anymore, I would consume the occasional remains from the jackals that I came across.

"One morning a herd of zebra came grazing near where I was lying. The sight of the colts sent old belly into violent screams and protests and my mouth started to water. But belly had overestimated himself. He had eaten so much of me, I would have had trouble killing even the smallest newborn colt if it had danced in front of my snout. So, while belly mumbled and slobbered, I watched the zebras eating grass and I thought to myself…why not? Wrapping my dripping tongue around a bunch of the stuff, I started chewing. It didn't taste like anything and was stringier than jackal meat, but at least it was something. Old belly let up when he noticed the chewing. I guess he hadn't figured out yet what it was and was looking forward to a chunk of zebra. When that grass dropped in on him, he was so surprised he just threw it all back out and growled and grumbled like he was going to take off on his own and leave me behind. He took an extra large chomp of my insides.

"I realized this was the moment where we would have to decide who was king. At first I blamed it all on the old man. I would have eaten him all over again if I'd had the chance, snapping each sinew through my teeth twice before I swallowed it. When he caught me thinking such thoughts, belly relaxed and began to whisper that we'd show that old sucker who was king of the plains. But when belly whispered 'king', I knew he was talking about himself, not me, and sure enough he began to lash about and send down lightning bolts from his hunger throne. I stuffed another wad of grass into him, this one less chewed than the first, and when he growled I fed him another and another. We wrestled, growling and snarling at one another. The zebras in the distance, frightened by the noise of our struggle, fled. At last old belly had no more strength to reject the grass and lay exhausted. I too, no less than he. Toward sunset I dragged myself to the water hole and drank until we both threatened to burst. But I had won. I was king of belly. Oh, from time to time he would lash out at me with his hunger whip, but the threat of balls of grass quickly brought him to grumbling obedience.

"I soon admitted, however, I could not live on grass. It came out as it went in and with pains as great or greater than those of belly's hunger whip. I noticed the mice who scattered around me carrying seeds and nuts and I began to try seeds. Some were bitter, others were tasteless, but they had more substance than the grass. I observed the monkeys who were eating fruits in the trees at the edges of the plain and I started picking up what they dropped or what I could get by jumping against the trees. Occasionally a little monkey would fall when I sprang against a tree and then there would be a terrible chattering above while the adults pelted me with fruits. Belly, when he sensed a little monkey on the ground before me, would growl and tear at my insides, but his hunger whip had lost its force and the little one would clamber unmolested back up to its mother. The adults became accustomed to my presence and, though they still pelted me with fruit, they chattered less and less at my approach. It was almost as if they understood I had mastered belly and meant them no harm.

"Though my hunger was controlled at last in this fashion, my body did not adjust well – great chunks of hair fell out, my mane lost its sheen, my tail still resembles the naked protuberance of a rat, my teeth broke on the seeds and nuts. My gums bleed. But I am king at last of belly, unmoved by his occasional begging for the tiniest morsel of mouse or baby monkey. In a sense, that is what led to my capture. When men found me, I had lost all feeling for them. Like the fruits and roots I ate, I was indifferent and unaware of the pit they had prepared for me. So, my friend, when they release us both in the arena tomorrow, although they've starved me since I got here, you have nothing to be afraid of. I will look for seeds, maybe some dried fruits…grass even will do if nothing else is available."

"No! No! My soul demands you shred me, tear me into little chunks, suck my eyeballs from their sockets, shred my entrails and toss them into the air…catching them on the down drop with hideous slurping noises. And all the while my soul will forgive you for releasing it from its fleshly prison. Snap the bones at their joints, tear out the cartilage, I won't resist. I'll continue to pray for you until you have crushed the last breath from my gaping, wounded chest and torn my bleeding heart from my breast with your hideous claws. And even as my soul soars heavenward, borne by angels singing praises for my unwavering courage in the presence of your terrible onslaught, I will still plead that when Beelzebub drags you off to hell and flays your monstrous hide from your monstrous bones that you be forgiven, even though you must spend all eternity roasting in hell fire and torment!"

"You're beginning to sound more and more like belly. Maybe, if you'd try eating grass…"

"Son of Satan, it's all a trick! You want to surprise me, lull me, to confuse the heavenly hosts when they descend for my soul, and so rescue your own miserable hide from the terrible torments that await you. But you're wrong…I am going to paradise, directly to paradise and meet Jesus and Peter and Paul and you are going to send me there when you squeeze my lifeblood out of my body and set my soul free. And from paradise I will come riding back with the heavenly hosts, armed with rods of iron and swords of fire, and we shall scourge the earth and crush all the demons and unbelievers and idolaters together with their idols…and all the creatures of

Satan shall be confounded as we fling him from his throne!" As he spoke, small flecks of foam gathered at the corners of his mouth and the leg chain hummed a dance against the floor.

"I'm not sure I understand your paradise and angels and devils and demons and satans thing. But maybe tomorrow we can search together at the end of the arena for seeds."

The winter sun ruled an auspicious sky. The Emperor Diocletian and his host, surrounded by worshipping local citizens, made sacred prayers to the sun and observed the public rituals asking Mithra's blessing upon the Emperor and the festive crowd semicircled in the arena.

The iron doors of the retaining chamber swung wide and a great, if rather older and worn looking, lion stalked blinking at the day into the arena, looking around as though seeking either prey or an exit. The crowd was hushed by the presence of the great beast, paralyzed in anticipation of the terrible and grisly pleasure that awaited them. Then a human being, the half-naked sacrificial victim, ran into the arena. Freed now from his chains, he raced up to the lion, raised his hands and eyes heavenward and began to call upon the heavenly hosts to witness his terrible martyrdom and the blood guilt that would now be on the assembled audience in general and the Emperor in particular.

The lion, ignoring the praying figure, sauntered over to the edge of the arena where several clumps of small white late-blooming daisies grew, and began nibbling them. The victim ran after him, his arms still upraised in supplication. This time he knelt beside the beast. The crowd held its breath – certainly the terrible moment had come. The great beast now lay down on its haunches and, like a cow chewing its cud, continued to masticate the daisies. The victim grabbed the lion's tail and tried to raise it to its feet. The lion ignored the indignity.

Not succeeding with pulling the tail, the victim tried to force one of his hands into the beast's mouth. The lion simply turned its head, rose and walked to another patch of daisies farther on, settled on its haunches, and munched the flowers.

Then, with amazing suddenness, the bloodletting for which the crowd had come commenced. With terrible screams, roaring, gnashing of teeth, and rending and shredding of flesh the slaughter began! And when it was over, all that remained of the lion were a mangled paw, some hairs from the mane, and chunks of hide scattered over the entire arena. The victim lay writhing where he had fallen in the center of the arena, choking, breathless in his attempts to swallow the last of the bony tail.

Chroniclers of the time report that Diocletian is said to have found the performance 'interesting' and certainly better than the 'dog-piling' for which some of the German tribes were noted. But one young man clearly grasped what he had seen, and understood its implications, which, as the Roman general and emperor, Constantine I, he would put into practice at the battle of Milvian Bridge over the Tiber in 312 – abandoning the Sun God and Mithra for the all-powerful warrior, Jesus of the Christians.

An account of this momentous event is given by the Church historian of the day, Eusebius, who knew Constantine and assures us that the Emperor swore that this was indeed what happened at Milvian Bridge, where he prayed to God and was answered by a most marvelous sign of the cross. And later, in a dream, he was told to conquer his enemies in Jesus' name. From that time on the Emperor ruled as a Christian monarch should, slaying the foes of God, who were now his foes, including his son and wife and fellow emperor Licinius, and rewarding the friends of God, who were now his friends, including Eusebius and those bishops allied with him.[5]

The History and Development
of Modern Flap Techniques

Prologue

The Indian law code, the *Laws of Manu*, makes it clear that each human 'self' is an individual alone unto itself in that it is born alone, dies alone, and ultimately enjoys alone the rewards and punishments its has earned while alive.[1]

This condition is so because, according to the *Katha Upanisad*, in the beginning "The Self-Existent made the senses turn outward. Accordingly, man looks toward what is without, and sees not what is within. Rare is he who, longing for immortality, shuts his eyes to what is without and beholds the Self."[2]

(A Draft for the Journal of World Science)

George M. Goodworth, Ph.D.
Frank S. Hollingwood, M.D.

The earliest attempts to replace a portion of the abdominal wall in mammals with a section of glass so that, in the interests of science, the behavior of the inner organs could be more closely monitored were not successful for several reasons. The pane was difficult to seal. It was necessarily small because it entailed a structural weakening. The glass could not give when the organism moved and so had a tendency in extreme situations to slip. The work was restricted to larger, fairly inactive animals, (e.g., cows and older horses under sedation). Lighting consisted of a single beam projected in from an external source. The animals were subject to an unusual amount of breakage. Costs were prohibitive. The data gained of questionable merit.

Such projects had almost been discontinued when the advent of the new plastics and radical developments in transistor technology made them possible on a vastly more sophisticated plane. The new plastics are flexible, are practically indestructible, do not cloud, and as Prof. G. P. Prosit of the University of British Columbia, Institute of Northern Animal Research points out, "…properly implanted, they provide a degree of strength and support far surpassing the original tissue walls."[i]

With the implantation of extremely small power cells generating their current from the digestive energies of an active stomach, an unlimited current supply can be assured from within the organism. A single glass of milk, fortified with glucose, can "provide enough illumination to read a book of approximately eighty pages of large roman type."[ii]

Probably the most exciting aspect of the new materials and techniques is that they make possible 'flaps' in internal organs as well as in the abdominal wall; i.e. flaps within flaps (e.g., a flap in the abdominal wall followed by one in some member/s of the digestive tract).

From sedated quadrupeds, scientists have been able to move to lower primates and, of course, finally to man. The first volunteers in these research programs were brave young men from medical schools, the homeless lured by high compensation and assurances their flaps would be maintained alive in solution and restored intact at the end of the experiments, and conscientious objectors

---

i. G. P. Prosit, <u>Abstracts in Biology</u>, September 1995, p. 197. He continues on page 204 "…new implant techniques make larger windows possible and leak proof. The most violent internal hemorrhage remains absolutely dripless." He foresees a time when "…we may find it most practicable to replace the greater portion of worn-out bodies with these superior materials."

ii. Ibid., p. 206.

who were selected by the government to fulfill their military service obligations in this manner.[iii]

For reasons that still are not completely understood, the conservation of monkey flaps is less difficult than that of human flaps. Monkey flap survival percentages are significantly higher. Figures released from the University of Colorado Medical Center for 15 cases each of chimpanzee and human flap removals showed an 83% flap recovery for the chimpanzees as compared to a 47% flap recovery for the human subjects.[iv] This can be expressed in a flap deterioration graph as follows:

- - - - - - - -

INSERT GRAPH 1 A

- - - - - - - -

A further examination of these two groups as represented in the above graph reveals that this not an expression of a clear one to one ratio as Nasserbett and Boyle[v] have pointed out; i.e., 12.45 chimpanzee flaps and 7.05 human flaps. The reason for this is that

---

iii. A report by John M. Richardson in the <u>American Medical Journal</u>, 32:91, June 1994, p.64 ff., discusses the interesting case of one such individual recruited from an urban renewal project in Chicago who, informed that his flap had died and been discarded, refused to permit surgeons to remove the valuable electronic measuring devices they had affixed to his kidneys and bladder. Because of the legal complexities involved, he was reimbursed and released with the instruments. He returned to the area from which he had been recruited and shortly thereafter was brought into a hospital emergency room, the victim apparently of an internal rupture occasioned by a combination of alcohol saturation and a short in one of the power cells.

iv. P. P. Barnes and J. P. Nobbe, "A comparative study of human and chimpanzee flap survival", <u>The Colorado Medical Center Quarterly Review of Medicine</u>, 116:21, March-April 1992, pp. 39-42.

v. B. M. Nasserbett and T. A. Boyle, "A study of a comparative study of human and chimpanzee flap survival", <u>Journal of Modern Biology</u>, 3:33, September 1993, p. 37ff.

in the case of one chimpanzee 45% of his flap could be grafted and consequently recovered, and in the case of one of the human subjects only 5% of the flap was recoverable. The subjects in all cases were male so there was no significant sex differential between them. As a matter of secondary concern, it was noted that in a number of chimpanzees there was a marked increase in same gender preference after the flaps were replaced.

Subsequent improvements in technique and storage solution preparation at the University of Colorado Medical Center coupled with postoperative massage therapy on the restored flaps then narrowed considerably the discrepancy between the two groups as is reflected in the following chart:[vi]

- - - - - - - - -

(INSERT GRAPH 1 B)

- - - - - - - -

These figures also indicate that there was a considerable increase in flap conservation in all subjects due to the addition of testosterone/estrogen in varying amounts to the solutions at intervals for up to 96 hours after initial flap removal. This increase for the human subjects expressed itself in an increase in what is termed "portion-survival", or "PS", and not in "total-survival", or "TS"; i.e., there was not an appreciable increase in the recovery of individual flaps in their entireties, but rather in the recovery of larger portions of single flaps in individual cases.

Another interesting aspect of subsequent study of the hormone addition to the storage solutions was its effect on the shapes of the "PS" flaps. If estrogen alone was added, there was a marked predominance of parallelograms over other forms, though the amount added seemed to have no significant effect on a scale ranging from 1:1,000,000 to 100:1,000,000. If testosterone was added alone, then triangles were dominant. In a study done at the Mayo Clinic on fourteen male chimpanzees in which the two hormones were

---

vi. P. P. Barnes and James Gribble, "A further comparative study of human and chimpanzee flap survival," <u>Colorado Medical Center Quarterly Review of Medicine</u>, 130:16, December-January 1989-1990, pp. 15-18.

added in equal amounts simultaneously there were five cases of "TS" and nine cases of "PS".[vii] Of the latter, three were pentagons, four were squares, one was an octagon, and one a heptagon. Neither parallelograms nor triangles appeared.[viii]

- - - - - - - - -

(INSERT GRAPH 2 A)

- - - - - - - - -

It is obvious that the various flap shapes complicate the surgical restoration of the surviving section, necessitating either skin and muscle transplants from other portions of the anatomy or partial restoration with permanent plastic fillers. Later lay interest in the possibility of flap replacement has altered this difficulty radically. This interest by the general public has brought with it an entirely new phase in the development and use of flap surgery.

There are several reasons for this interest, both on the part of the layperson and the surgeon. Today the plastics are more durable than the original abdominal wall. Of particular appeal to many persons confronted with weight problems and certain kinds of ruptures is the fact that the plastics, though flexible, do not stretch as human tissue does; therefore a firm waist can be maintained indefinitely with the plastics permanently inserted, eliminating the need for braces or other such devices. This is especially true of newer implant techniques, which permit the laminating of thin vertical strips on a horizontal film. These strips then act very much like abdominal muscles and can actually be shaded with a toner that gives the whole a certain 'muscular appearance'. Connected on all sides to the muscle pattern they can be expanded and contracted as easily as these, with the advantage that they always return to and

---

vii. George C. Wilcox, "The use of hormones and flap recovery", Howard Journal of American Medical Studies, 12:91, p. 861ff.

viii. In none of the studies cited here did other than straight line figures occur. P. Smith, M.D., of the University of Utah, writing in Modern Medicine 38:151, November 1992, p. 588ff., later found that if the solution was kept at a constant 101° Fahrenheit (a fever temperature for normal tissue), then curvilinear alterations occasionally occurred.

maintain their original shape. Here there is no problem in keeping the severed tissue alive for later recovery because the plastic is a permanent substitute. This in turn means the complicated and costly process of tissue maintenance can be eliminated, and the individual has a more durable abdominal wall than before.

To what degree various social factors influence the general public's decision to undergo flap removal is difficult to determine. However, as the following graph illustrates, the operations are performed primarily in certain religious and economic groups, according to Bromberg.[ix]

- - - - - - - - -

(INSERT GRAPH 2 B)

- - - - - - - - -

Certainly one of the most relevant aspects of the general increase in the use of the plastic flap implant is a vastly improved diagnostic possibility for the specialist in internal medicine. A cursory examination of internal color conditions, general organ tone, fatty tissue accumulations, etc., can be performed with no more inconvenience after the initial operation than removal of the patient's garments.

Of course there are certain psychological and sociological consequences of flap surgery. These have been studied in great depth already: Blanders and Whitson: "The gestalt approach to specific forms of anxiety following flap surgery", American Journal of the Gestalt Society, 981:12, January 1989, pp. 35ff; Whitson and Collins: "Flap surgery and deviant behavior", Psychology, Sociology and Medicine, 19:8, June 1996, pp. 165ff; A. M. Brunsworth: "Marital relations and flap surgery, a sociological study," New England Journal of Sociology, December 1998, pp. 65ff; to name a few.

Some of these consequences are worth noting briefly here. For example, one of the most widely observed sociological effects is on the selection of a marriage partner. Individuals who have a plastic

---

ix. Howard Huett Bromberg, "Social factors influencing flap surgery", University of Chicago Quarterly for Social and Religious Research, 99:831, June 1992, p. 16.

abdominal wall often limit their choice of partner to others with the same condition. One explanation for this phenomenon, according to Williams and Williams, et al.,[x] is that apparently the unilateral visibility of the internal organs has an inhibiting effect during sexual intercourse.

Another aspect of extensive use of flap replacement, with limited, though interesting psychological consequences, is what has been referred to as the "TV syndrome", so called by Johnson and Bentwell who first studied and analyzed it in Nature and Science.[xi]

As Johnson and Bentwell point out in their study, in certain rare cases where individuals demonstrate tendencies toward mental abnormalities ranging from schizophrenia to paranoia, the flap transplant is of considerable secondary benefit, arresting almost immediately in these cases the progress of the mental illness. Though in rare instances individuals have then developed "TV syndrome"; i.e., an obsessive preoccupation with the viewing of their own internal organs through the plastic flap. Only in a few of these instances, however, has said obsession interfered with these individuals leading normal lives.

In conclusion then, one has in the development of flap surgery a clear illustration of the progress which science makes from the limited plane of the experimental to the wider one of general application for the benefit of all mankind, a path historically followed by all significant contributions to new knowledge.

———————

George M. Goodworth, Ph.D., takes the unfinished last page from the printer. The final draft is almost ready. He reads what he has just typed – "TV syndrome". He and Frank have argued over the implications of some of Johnson and Bentwell's data. An individual could certainly be keenly interested in observing his internal organs...say as a medical student, a physiologist, or a

———————

x. W. Williams et al., "Flap replacement and the marriage bed", Marriage Counselor International, 6:6, June 1993, p. 55ff.

xi. Johnson, Johnson and Robert Bentwell, "The TV syndrome", Nature and Science, 191:37, pp. 56-81.

scientist. But that doesn't necessarily imply mental aberrations! This is one of the problems of the social sciences in general…they are quick to confuse theory with fact…too often all theory and no fact! Conclusions drawn before the studies…anything but scholarly. Probably should add some sort of precautionary footnote on the study, if Frank is amenable. There isn't much time…it's got to be finished by the first of April.

The article is well written and reasonably scholarly. They have been assured in advance there will be no difficulty in placing it in the *Journal of World Science* once it is done.

Earlier in the day he had telephoned Frank about minor changes in the text, grammatical mostly. Frank was certainly excited. For him it might go a long way toward getting him out of City Hospital and into the State Medical Center.

George turns the computer off, places the neat, unpaginated sheets into the top left drawer of the desk and lights a cigar. The heavy smell quickly rids the room of its predecessors' stale scents. George's long fingers stop their nervous agitations against his thumbs as the cigar relaxes his system.

George is a scholar of the first magnitude. He enjoys the absolute respect of his colleagues. A brilliant cross between philosopher and biologist, he moves from conference to conference reading papers, followed everywhere by eager disciples and publication requests.

George's relationship with Frank, as with all of his associates, is like his relationship with his work, businesslike and professional. He does not mix friendship with scholarship. Mutual interest in mutual scientific problems, yes, but no one among his colleagues is allowed too near the ambitions and thoughts of the real, inner George. Before one is aware of it, somebody is trying to claim credit where it's not due. It can even happen unintentionally.

He stops pacing and heads for the bathroom, closes the door. The full-length mirror swings to confront him. For several seconds he stares at himself in the glass…nervous as hell, his fingers doing such a war dance on the thumbs that even he notices it. The cigar is out and he's eating it. "Pfuii!" he spits the mess into the toilet and closes the top, forgetting to flush. He stares at his reflection again.

George isn't a lonely man, not at all. Apart from his circle of colleagues, he has friends, close friends. But he keeps them ignorant of his work – a habit he picked up working at Fort Dietrich on 'chemical/biological warfare' projects for Defense. Too many people don't understand. Friends are there for friendship. With friends one talks trivia, ignores the great problems of science. Friends chatter on and on about insignificant things. The conversation can be cut by the yard…how they've slept, attacks of 'indigestion', ills, pains, creaks, squeaks…as though these were the most fascinating things in the world. The sorts of things his professional associates would probably ridicule, like arguments about the value of herb teas, folk remedies, water diets, positions of the stars, and one's constitution…and the value of massive doses of vitamin C for colds "like some scientist said." He arbitrates disputes over herb teas and is an all-around good listener.

His colleagues aren't his friends and his friends aren't his colleagues. He imagines a party where everybody from both sides were to be present…they would bore one another flat…or maybe worse, his associates would try to turn his friends into 'objects of scientific study'. He knows a couple of bio-sociologists who go in for that sort of thing. One cannot combine the two worlds without compromising one or the other, or both.

So efficiently does he separate them that his colleagues assume they are his friends and that George is just a 'cold fish'. They would not believe he has another existence in which his intimates know nothing of him as a scholar, author of profound papers, chairman of international committees, that he lives another life where the parameters of interest are almost animal…food, drink, petty jealousies, gossip.

One of the major attractions of this separation is that the inhabitants of the two universes can in no way threaten one another or his role in either place. "All right, I'm coming." He has kept them apart, almost, and that is what bothers him now. His friends want to meet in his apartment over drinks to discuss that damned paper.

At a party a week ago where everybody was smashed, he had carelessly dropped a hint that he was working on a valuable analysis that would be appearing in the *Journal of World Science*. They certainly didn't know what the *JWS* was, but the words 'scientific' and 'world' got them excited. It was careless, and just when he thought it had been forgotten they made him promise to invite them all to a "reading". And they wouldn't understand a word of it!

He removes his trousers and shirt and drapes them over the towel bar. Puts on his terry cloth dressing gown over his shorts and T-shirt and moves back into the living room and starts setting up so they will have places to sit when they come in. Puts a bottle of good brandy out…they like his brandy. Tidies up the ashtrays. Checks the cube trays. There are enough, unless the evening goes all night. He'll have to remember to fill them when they're empty.

Another turn through the apartment…as tidy as one can expect from a bachelor. There are snacks in the fridge, plenty to drink. Still he's uneasy. How will they react? And what if they make more demands on him? They're his friends, but his friends because they have nothing to do with his work. "Oh hell! It's almost time."

He returns to the bathroom to get ready, closes the door again. For a few seconds the phrasing of a sentence in the paper bothers him and he tries to rework it in his head. A loud knocking disturbs his train of thought. There they are. His hands begin their agitated dance. Finally he smiles the relaxed smile he keeps for them and removes his T-shirt. In the past he has always gone to their places, and he realizes he should have had them to the apartment a long time ago. The clear plastic of his abdominal wall reflects into the mirror.

"Just a minute, just a minute! You want to beat the door down? Must be the brandy smell." He is kidding and proud at the same time. He almost admits to himself that he wants to impress them, almost laughs out loud at the coming ego trip as he turns to the sink to eject a fresh razor blade.

"Everything's ready. Just let me finish up here and get to the door if you will, there's enough for everybody!" The fingers that have dealt so deftly with hundreds of specimens begin as deftly opening the plastic door…and his friends crowd into the apartment.

When Siva Lost His Cool

Prologue

It was a terrible age 1,095 years after the birth of Jesus – Christian knight pillaged and plundered and slew Christian knight. Peasants fled from these knightly conflicts into the dark forests where wild beasts devoured their women and children. The roofs of the churches sagged and leaked. Priests and monks and nuns ignored their vows of celibacy. The Holy City, Jerusalem, was in the hands of Muslims. At the end of that century Pope Urban II had a vision and called the knights of all Europe to take part in a great Crusade to liberate the Holy Land and to cease selling their strength and battle fury for vile pay. He challenged those who lusted for blood and washed their hands in Christian blood to redirect their blood lusts and go and wash their hands in the blood of the unbelievers, to cease being soldiers of Hell at home and go to become soldiers of God. He commanded them to wear upon their armor and other accoutrements the Cross of Christ. And should they perish, they would be dying there where Jesus had died and ascended into Heaven, and this would be their own eternal reward for such a consecrated end.[1]

Unfortunately, those Believers who were to be used as an alternative blood supply for washing knightly hands scoffed at these unbelievers who worshipped a deity 'divided into three parts' and credited with fathering a baby with a human female. For those Believers there will always be but one God, Allah, the Good and the Merciful, whose Prophet is Mohammed.

The *Koran* assured them that the perversions of the Jew and the Christian could never prevail over the Warriors of Allah.[2] The *Holy Koran* makes it clear that there are only two categories of warrior: those Believers who fight for Allah and so exchange the life of this world for the reward of that other, and those who are disbelievers and fight for idols. The latter are the servants of the devil and they shall be overcome.[3] However, Believers are not to begin the conflicts in this war, but when it comes they are to fight with Allah against all those who are against them, to slay them wherever they may be found, and to drive them from the places they have taken.[4]

THE TIME: Midwinter 1097-1098 at the siege of Antioch during the First Crusade.
THE PLACE: A dusky, cavernous chamber containing vaguely recognizable human shapes queued in a long line zigzagging back and forth upon itself...

A low moaning hangs in the air. Enough light escapes around a door at the head of the line to permit individuals to recognize one another more clearly, and here a heated argument begins as two figures recognize one another: Conrad, the Crusader Bishop of Metz, and Ibn el Shama, 'Sword of Islam' and defender of Antioch. Both have been slain in a midnight sortie of the Turks into the Franks camped under the leadership of Bohemond. Wedged sideways in the helmet of the bishop is the silver-handled scimitar of the 'Sword of Islam'. In the helmet of the 'Sword of Islam', wedged sideways, is the Bishop's broadsword with a jeweled cross upon its hilt.

"Infidel dog! Do you know what is behind this door? It is the great testing! Beyond this door waits the Archangel Gabriel with his terrible questions and his fiery tongs. Your worthless soul will be placed upon his judgment scales, and when your nefarious deeds outweigh what little good you might have done once as a baby, you will be dumped without ceremony into the place of the eternal flame, where your backside will be roasted off and renewed and roasted off again forever!"

"Ha, barbarian whore's son! Beyond that door is truly the great testing, but it is St. Peter who administers the exams with his blessed iron flail, and he will flail you for what you are. He will need no weighing instruments. Your foul blasphemies precede you! He will fling you into the burning pit where the worm dies not and the fire never goes out!"

"Infidel, it is Mohammed himself who stands there with a flaming sword waiting for your head to remove it and pitch it willy-nilly into the place of eternal torments!"

"Devil's seed, it is Jesus who stands there with Mohammed gift wrapped in chains, and he will bind him about your scrawny Saracen's neck and drop you from the skies into the hot place!"

"Dog's excrement, it is Allah who shall seize you by your worthless infidel's ears and drag you to the brink of hell and boot you in! And good riddance!"

"Begetter of lies, it is the Trinity itself that waits there in its tripartite splendor to scorch the soles of your pagan feet and to roast your pagan soul."

This discussion might have continued indefinitely had not the narrow door gradually opened and a powerful voice commanded them both to enter. There was some jostling, of course, for first place, and the weapons lodged in their respective heads clanged against one another like steel antlers of wild beasts engaged in battle. For a moment their clanging quieted the moaning in the cavern. Then, as quickly as it began, their struggle ended...

"Infidel dog, it is your doom that awaits therein, enter first, that you may first taste the punishments for your nauseating and most disgusting acts."

"Pagan defiler of the Holy Places, anathema of God and Man, you enter first to receive your miserable sentence. This will give the blessed angels and Peter and Paul time to remove your stinking carcass to its final resting place before I, a Crusader, go in!"

What had been a struggle for precedence became one for post-sequence, which was resolved only when a second narrow door appeared in the wall next to the first, and both great men could enter simultaneously, each turning sideways to accommodate the weapon lodged firmly in his skull.

Beyond the door was neither Mohammed nor Jesus, neither Jehovah nor Allah, neither Peter nor Gabriel, but the Beginning of the world, Brahma, placidly dozing on a cushion with eyes shut against the bright light of what seemed to be the open sky. Standing beside the Beginning of the world was the Ending of the world, Siva, gently swaying with four arms weaving about head and body like hand-headed serpents. Pacing back and forth before the Beginning and Ending of time was the world's Maintainer and Preserver, Vishnu as Krishna the 'chariot driver'. It was he who had summoned them to enter and who now spoke:

"Gentlemen, as you are aware, I am sure, we are now in the Kali-Yuga, the final Yuga in which truth stands on but one of its four legs. Perhaps we are even on this Yuga's downside. Unfortunately, my colleague here feels we are at its closing and the last leg is buckling. He wants to begin his ending dance at once. I find his argument compelling, but not completely convincing. In all modesty, I believe I can maintain the world yet a while. In great part his argument rests upon both of your sacred texts, which prophesy a terrible destruction pending in a linear time. He believes your struggles in the names of your gods, both in their nature and magnitude, represent a common, though disharmonious, appeal on both your parts to end as expeditiously as possible this Kali-Yuga so that the Great Brahma then can dream that dream which creates all anew and, having dreamed it, open his eyes so that the cosmic light of the dream emanates forth again. But, I am not sure you are both crying for the end of the world, that you are united in the single wish for the closing of the Yuga. Rather, from my experiences among humans as a warrior and charioteer, I sense that you seek something less, seek only each for the end of the other. If this is the case, then you wish only that which man has always seemed to wish – to live himself, but to see his fellow perish. This is a simple and normal human desire and I can maintain the balance of the whole for a while longer. So, my human friends, what is your pleasure? Speak!"

Of course, the two great warriors were stunned. Most of what had been said made no sense. Brahma did look a bit like God, although without a beard, and this speaker could be Gabriel or St. Peter...but the character with the four arms was something else again. Besides, nothing in their tradition had prepared either of them for this – a god who asked such questions.

"Blessed St. Peter or St. Paul or St. John or St. Andrew, forgive me for not recognizing you. Certainly the end will come in Jehovah's own good time, but what we Christian Crusaders desire now is the end of the pagan rogue who tramples upon the Lord's birthplace and charges admission to the tomb and refers to the Church of the Resurrection as the 'dung heap'."

"O great Gabriel, the end is Allah's, as was the beginning. We seek only in your name to spread the word as commanded by you to Mohammed in Allah's glorious *Koran*. We seek to show the infidel the perversity of his path, and to end the blasphemies which proclaim Allah to be a three-part schizophrenic having babies and consorting with young virgins."

"Listen to him not, o blessed Saint! He is a heathen. His wicked kind mutilate their bodies with the accursed Jew's circumcision. They rape and pillage and plunder Christian homes, destroy Christian family values. And they wear silk undergarments and perfume their bodies and enslave young boys and girls and let homosexuals into their armies."

"Hearken not to the infidel's perfidious polytheistic ravings. They are the unclean scum of the earth. They pollute their bodies with alcohol and where swine eat filth, this filth eats swine. With the same mouth they claim to drink your blood and eat your body. They feast on human flesh as well – see how the Satanist Bohemond roasts the bodies of the faithful upon spits before the wall of Antioch as food for his devil hordes."

"Ignore the slanders of these liars who fling on their catapults the heads of Christian martyrs over the walls of the cities sacred to you, which we have liberated in Jesus' name. They loot the bodies of fallen Christian knights and sell the living into slavery. They pee upon the cross and into the sacred utensils. There is no infamy to which these followers of Lucifer will not stoop."

"Pay these demon locusts no mind. They wade knee-deep in the blood of your righteous ones, the people of Allah and the people of his Prophet. They stink of garlic and sweat and believe washing their bodies to be a grievous sin. In summer they smell worse alive than dead. They say their perfidious prayers with unwashed hands and feet. They catapult severed heads of the soldiers of Allah into the cities that they besiege."

"Enough, gentlemen, and thank you for your input.

"You see, my dear friend and colleague, it is but a case of what in their minds passes for knowledge and religious commitment or holy war. It is certainly not serious enough to warrant a new beginning. Let us simply return them through karma's wheel, that they may continue their diversions awhile."

The Bishop spoke first, with such feeling that the scimitar rattled against his helm. "But I have been promised paradise! My sins are in remission, my soul cleansed by this great Crusade! Here…I have the sacred indulgence that the blessed Holy Father Urban who looses and binds on earth and in heaven gave me. I demand to see this pagan flung into the pit and my soul clothed in a new body."

For the first time, the Ending of the world spoke, and stretching out one of his hands he asked to see the slip of parchment that the Bishop held. "No!" cried the Bishop as a hand snaked in his direction. "You are a demon! Angels do not come with four arms!"

Suddenly the parchment burst into flame and was consumed. At this the Bishop shrank back, which emboldened the 'Sword of Islam' who, seeing all as Allah's, realized that this strange angel or jinn must be Allah's too. From his inner garment he retrieved the folded and worn leather scrap upon which had been engraved the promise of the 57th *Surah*: "Now when ye meet in battle those who disbelieve, then it is a smiting of the necks…And those who are slain in the way of Allah, He rendereth not their actions vain." As the fourth hand extended toward it, the leather scrap too burst into flame.

"It is time," said the Ending of the world. "I shall dance and Brahma dream. Step aside."

"No! They are little children. To end the Yuga now, because of their 'human squabbles', is ridiculous! Their blood and bones fertilize the ground, their puny swords and iron suits rust away; still nature thrives, flowers bloom, trees grow, the world itself breathes and lives and its breath is sweet. Let us wait yet a short time, say a thousand years or so, to see. A thousand years is but a thousandth of a thousandth of a thousandth of the lifetime of a single spark emerging from Brahma's eye. So brief is it that such a spark would only travel a thousandth of a thousandth of a thousandth of a single eyelash of Brahma before its extinction. Permit me to maintain it for a thousand years more. Then we shall see."

The weaving hands of the Ending of the world stopped their dance and clasped themselves in pairs behind his back as he considered this possibility.

"Agreed, but upon one condition. The mighty law of karma demands they be returned, and this is my condition, O Preserver and Maintainer. In every other birth they shall change places, the Christian be reborn a Muslim and the Muslim a Christian and then back again. And in every fifth rebirth, each shall be born a Jew."

"For a thousand years then," agreed Vishnu, "they shall change places and then we shall reconvene our congress here."

A smile played faintly on Siva's face for, as cosmic dancer, he realized that in men hate travels unabated and concentrates like heavy metal in the soul from birth to rebirth. Now this hatred of each for the other would in generation after generation also turn Christian against Christian, Muslim against Muslim, and Jew against Jew, each against his kind ever more intensely to a thousand year crescendo that even Vishnu could not resist, a crescendo within whose fury nature too must cease to live and breathe.

And perhaps there was an echo of Siva's smile on the placid face of Brahma, who may already have begun to mediate upon the new dream he would dream...or perhaps not.

The Zoo

Prologue

In *Genesis* 2:19-20, we read that in the beginning

> "...out of the ground the Lord God formed every beast
> of the field, and every fowl of the air; and brought
> *them* unto Adam to see what he would call them: and
> whatsoever Adam called every living creature, that *was*
> the name thereof. And Adam gave names to all cattle,
> and to the fowl of the air, and to every beast of the
> field; but for Adam there was not found an help meet
> for him."

Wise Pliny, the Elder, in his discussion of the ways of men,
women, and animals, claims that the traveler Durius reports of
human beings in India who (unlike Adam, who remained faithful
to his kind) form unions with beasts, and the offspring of these
unions are half human and half animal. In other parts of India some
men are born with hairy tails while others are covered entirely by
their ear flaps. He marvels, as one must, at these wonderful 'toys of
Nature', which Nature produces for her own entertainment.[1]

"A zoo is a wonderful thing," proclaimed the editor of the
conservative *Evening Star* in an address to the American Legion Post
1618. "There's not a father or a grandfather here in this audience
who would deny his child the educational experience of seeing wild

animals in cages. However, and I want to emphasize this 'however', the City Council's plans do not call for such a normal, healthy, educational zoo!

"The Council wants a park in which all kinds of wild and ferocious beasts can roam about restricted only by a thin, wire fence. Not only will the lives of our women and children be in danger if, against better judgment, they wander into this horde of lions and camels and pythons, they will also be threatened on the once-quiet streets of our town when these monsters out of darkest Africa break their fences and run amok!"

To this warning was added that of the president of the First National Bank. He objected, in a full-page ad taken at the bank's expense in the more liberal *Morning Star* for two weeks running, that six city blocks of rent and tax-paying tenements would be sacrificed for a project where only a nominal admission might be charged. The Rev. Howard M. Bradwicker, D.D., pastor of the Hope and Grace Tabernacle Tower, pointed out most clearly and emphatically to the Chamber of Commerce at its weekly prayer breakfast that he had visited many monkey houses in zoos across this great land of ours and there had witnessed the vile creatures doing the most despicable things – things that would perhaps have rendered a lesser warrior of God blind, or at least speechless, things that women and children should certainly not even dream about let alone be exposed to. And he absolutely refused to respond to the Chamber's vociferous gadfly Bill Warren's request for 'for instances'.

Mrs. Patterson-Crawley, who had subscribed to *National Geographic* for over thirty-five years, and who had always donated her old copies to the Public Library, assured her Garden and Canasta Club that she had read of unsuspecting individuals who had been devoured alive by crocodiles that had emerged from the toilet bowls in apartments and hotel rooms…and that in a place as civilized as New York City. As a result the Club members voted to protest at City Council meetings until they were assured there would be no crocodiles in the planned park.

A 'Mothers' League was organized. The PTA sponsored a debate between the principal of the William Smith, Jr. Junior

High School and Miss Allison Jones, resident authoress of some renown, who had written an entire book of animal poems entitled *A Book of Animal Poems*.

In favor of the zoo issue, it was pointed out that Federal funds would be available for razing the tenements and building the pens and cages. The Bank would also be adequately compensated for the taxable ground it was surrendering to the City. Of course, such a project would also create jobs, a not unimportant consideration after the layoffs that had followed the closure of the Markworth Slaughter House and Sausage Works by the State Health Inspectors. But it was a neighborhood battle between the 'Dudes' and the 'Dragons', in which two policemen and an old Czech grocer were injured, that finally tipped the scale toward planting wild animals where once wild juveniles had roamed and mugged their prey.

The City got its zoo. The animals, few and most of them older surplus from other zoos, remained inside their fences.

The toothless mountain lion gnawed lazily.

The balding zebra grazed leisurely.

A three-legged antelope limped lamely but gamely, and if one closed one's eyes, the sound of its hop conveyed an inexpressible sense of vast grasslands and ancient water holes.

Visitors often wrote on the survey sheets distributed at the gate as they exited that, except for the fences and the 'keep off the grass' signs, they felt they might have been on safari in the African plains. This illusion was heightened by little boys with air rifles pelleting each other and the zebra.

The warning of the editor of the *Evening Star* was forgotten as even the smallest of children wandered about the park unharmed…throwing stones at the birds, pushing rosy fingers tantalizingly through the lion's fence, making faces back at the monkeys. In the monkey house itself, a motorized curtain had been installed that could be activated at critical moments by any adult that happened to be present. The button for this mechanism had been installed high enough on the wall so that small children could not reach it, and when there were school tours, monkey movies were usually substituted for the monkeys themselves, who were locked in the back of their pen. Teenagers who, of course, could reach the button were encouraged to 'move on' by the attendant, a retired and nearsighted biology professor from City Community College who kept a close watch on monkeys and visitors alike.

———————————

The zoo had been open for eight months and twenty-one days when on the 3rd of April, late in the evening, the water buffalo bull broke through his fence and fled into town, where he spent the night cropping the flower beds and grazing the lilacs around the mayor's residence while the mayor's pedigreed and prize winning dog, 'Woofums', cringed barkless in the back of his kennel. Discovered the next morning, the buffalo was captured and quickly returned to his pen.

It wasn't until the beginning of June, however, that the full consequences of his escape came to light. The mayor's seventeen-year-old daughter was found 'to be with child'. Confronted with this fact by her parents, she broke into tears and admitted that she had had an 'arrangement' with the water buffalo on that infamous April night as she returned after midnight and slightly tipsy from a party. When asked why she hadn't said anything earlier, she wept and replied that she didn't think it would be so serious. Besides, she was afraid of what her parents would say to her drinking, and of what her friends might think of her. She could just hear that horrid Brenda Butterswort calling her 'buffalo gal'!

The housemaid probably put the story into circulation. In any case, the entire city had heard the tragic news within twenty-four hours. Everyone was sympathetic, even people who had voted against the mayor in the last election.

All of the anticipated horrors of the zoo were recalled and embellished. The Rev. Howard M. Bradwicker, D.D., pastor of the Hope and Grace Tabernacle Tower, emphasized to his congregation, and at the Chamber's prayer breakfast, that this was why God gave Adam dominion over the beasts and Eve, and ordered him to put them in cages...not Eve of course...he was to marry her and train her to love, honor, and obey.

Only Miss Allison Jones suggested, in a letter to the editor in the more liberal *Morning Star*, that the whole thing was unheard-of nonsense. However, soon thereafter, when the postman began to return autographed copies of her *Book of Animal Poems* together with caustic notes from outraged purchasers, she wrote the more liberal editor that indeed such things were rumored to happen in the vast wilds of the Indian Subcontinent, and suggested that the zoo be surrounded with a stone wall.

But the major issue now was the mayor's daughter and not the zoo. An abortion seemed the only plausible solution. Her physician refused to be responsible for her life should she be forced to carry the fruit of her womb to fullness.

However, the Bishop of the Diocese was not convinced of the necessity or even possibility of an abortion. "After all," he wrote to the Mayor in a personal letter, which was read aloud before Mass on successive Sundays, "we have before us a fertilized human egg. A thing of flesh and blood, heart and soul! Even if only half that soul is human, that half is sacred. To harm in any way that which Divine Providence has brought to be is to court eternal damnation!" He further insisted that it was not inconceivable that the Almighty had perhaps inflicted this tragedy upon the City in general and its Council and Mayor in particular as an admonition to struggle with all their energies against "Godless communism, licentiousness, and condoms," which had begun to infiltrate the high school where the young lady had less than diligently pursued her studies, and where Karl Marx's *Das Kapital* had recently been removed from the banned book list, while a copy of *The Catcher in the Rye* was placed where any senior could read it…a book which he understood clearly touted the so-called 'advantages' of the homosexual lifestyle.

On the other hand, Elder Smith of the Temple warned that the creature could have "cloven hooves" and held that "it might be better in the eyes of the Almighty in this unusual set of circumstances to destroy this 'half-devil' in the bud, so to speak." The Rev. Bubba Bob of the Fountain Full of Blood Ministries, which was conducting a revival in town at the time, proclaimed from his pulpit that though the young lady and the water buffalo had sinned in the eyes of God, the townsfolk should "hate the sin but love the sinner." No one was quite sure what this meant. Some believed it meant the young lady in question, who had now dropped out of high school, should be allowed to take a GED equivalency test for her high school diploma. Others thought he meant the water buffalo should be horsewhipped and fed to the mountain lion. This would have been a challenge of considerable proportions given the toothless nature of the latter.

But it was Bill Casey, son of the owner of the local American Motors Distributorship ("We are driven to drive you to drive us."), a close friend of the Mayor's daughter, and sometime juvenile delinquent, who possessed the courage necessary to act. He called at the Mayor's home and offered to marry the distraught young lady so that the poor cloven-hoofed seedling nesting in her womb would at least have a human father.

Her parents, who under other circumstances would have refused to let Bill in the door, consented with open arms. The daughter approved. They changed physicians. And the young couple began attending Mass regularly. An entire row of anti-Communist pamphlets appeared in the library on both sides of Karl Marx, and a copy of a little tract entitled *Sunbeams Do Not Sin* was mysteriously placed in all the elementary school kiddies' desks.

But, how mysterious indeed are the ways of the Spirit who "plants his footsteps upon the waves and rides upon the storm." A miracle was wrought in the womb of the Mayor's daughter. When on Christmas Eve, nine months after the tragedy, the unusual baby emerged, it was most usual. A facsimile of Bill Casey from the snub nose and blue eyes to the large hands and feet. Even the little hair it had was red like Bill's, though not twisted like his in dreadlocks. Of cloven hooves there was not a trace. It was certainly a sign of God's great grace and mercy. "A WONDER CHILD" wrote the liberal press. "A MIRACLE BABY" headlined the conservative. And Mrs. Parker, the supervising floor nurse for the Maternity Ward at the time, recalled, in an interview published in a number of papers, that the street lamp just outside her section window had distinctly brightened around midnight when the young lady went into labor.

That Christmas the tree lights at City Hall were brighter than ever, and the large papier-mâché animals gathered round the manger in the nativity scene down at the Water Works seemed somehow humbler and more subdued than usual, as though ashamed that one of their kind had crossed that divinely drawn line that separates men from beasts.

Only the water buffalo appeared completely unconcerned. He made not the least inquiry after his child. And when he died of stomach parasites a few months later, the town knew that a righteous sentence had been carried out by an unseen but omnipotent hand.

The Making of Presidents

Prologue

Aristotle, who believed with most of his contemporaries that thinking occurred in the heart and lungs area, held that the function of the brain was to temper the raging of the heart – to cool its heated thoughts. The brain itself was both fluid and solid. If it were too solid or too fluid, however, it could not perform its function properly. If it were too fluid, it would cause the blood to freeze, and if it were too solid, it would not cool the blood at all, resulting in sickness, madness, and death. It was this cooling function of the brain that accounted for the human male having more sutures in the skull than any other animal, even the female of the species.[1]

Peter Warton Woolsworth, like some Alaskan sled dog, arranges the world from eyes of different shades. An allergy has never let him conceal this fact with contact lenses. Peter and his lovely wife Ann were afraid their children too might be so defined, and postponed them for a full ten years of courage taking. But the children, six-year-old Fred and three-year-old Ann Marie, have the earthy brown eyes of their mother. Peter himself has ceased to be concerned by the quick start he gives people meeting him for the first time. However, he avoids looking into his own eyes in the mirror, concentrating instead on the slight scar on his upper lip left by a childhood sledding accident.

Peter and Ann are very much in love. Ann still curls her eyelashes afresh each day. They have lovely, bright children, a perky spayed Pekinese, a nice five bedroom house in a good neighborhood, and frequent promotions for Peter. It looked for a time as though they might have to move when PBM bought American Synthetics Inc., Peter's firm, but Peter was left in the home office, promoted, and put in charge of the then new and super secret PBM-American Synthetics Project.

The Project is no longer new nor secret, but PBM managed to get in early with a breakthrough that Peter himself engineered, and corner most of the English-speaking college and university market at a time when the financial situation of many institutions, even large, private universities, was catastrophic.

The Board at PBM had originally wanted to enter the textbook field and had made several tentative inquiries when they heard about American Synthetics and their work for the U.S. government during the Korean War. American had developed a completely dimensioned female 'companion', which could be packaged with C-rations and inflated as the soldier had leisure and loneliness. The government had ordered over 100,000 of them by the end of the war.

The Department of Defense had been delighted with the models. They were American girls. They prevented unnecessary contacts with the enemy. And they cut down on the disease rate in the front lines. The Department had asked American Synthetics to include prophylactics with its models so that GIs wouldn't get out of the habit of using these devices while 'up front' and then be in greater danger of disease while on leave in the population centers. Before the war ended American had a type on the drawing board that, employing the principle later developed for the auto safety belt, could not be comfortably used unless the prophylactic was in place. It contained a simple generating device that produced a sharp whistling sound and a spark when activated without the latex cover.

American had procured archetypes for its 'companions' from various racial, economic, and religious groups. A soldier could easily swap or save them the way children do with cowboy or airplane pictures from bubble gum wrappers. In addition to the basic design, every PX carried a line of American's 'inflatable modifiers' – kits that made an additional ten modifications possible, from eye and lip shades to certain pressure changes. In each model package for PX retail, American enclosed a simple questionnaire/warranty asking for preferences, suggestions, etc., and guaranteeing the item for one year with an unconditional replacement within the first thirty days and then a percentage toward the purchase of a new model on the remaining tread over the next eleven months. This gave American the base for one of the most advanced consumer research programs in the country. It was a program that was later imitated by everything from shaver companies to battery manufacturers.

During the Vietnam War American Synthetics, 'always in the forefront of finer, newer products', introduced a line of male counterparts for the women's service branches, and this a "long time before the women's lib business," as Peter often put it.

Of course these weren't the only things American produced. They weren't even their main line as far as gross sales and profits were concerned. They had subcontracts on napalm jelly and parts for phosphorus bombs that were considerably more important. But toward the end of the war, when PBM was looking around for a "marriage partner" as Peter's boss liked to say, it was this extensive experience with inflatable human substitutes that sold PBM on the merger with American rather than one of the textbook publishers.

When the serious merger discussions were first started, nobody at American could figure out what PBM wanted with American. Only after the lab facilities and plants had been thoroughly assessed by a team of engineers from PBM's San Francisco office, were Peter Woolsworth and two other engineers from the fabrics division called in to consult.

First Peter and his colleagues were promoted. Peter's salary more than doubled and he and Ann bought a boat and a new car. After they had been so bribed, they were sworn to secrecy by the head of the San Francisco team, a small, pudgy man named Gordon who wore a dark green plaid suit and had a nervous way of saying "relatively speaking" at the end of every third or fourth sentence. Gordon had a master's degree in 'educational psychology' and a Ph.D. in 'educational management systems analysis'.

Walter Benesch

"You see, it's this way, relatively speaking, that is, PBM views education as the wave of the future. That's where government funding is going...millions for adult basic education...continuing education...community colleges...post secondary opportunities...career ladder concepts...that's where local, state, and national governments are going to shoot the works, relatively speaking. People have more leisure. More unfilled needs for training, skill upgrading, expanded vocational interests...relatively speaking. Now, who's going to take care of all those consumers? Not the old-fashioned 'you-go-for-four-years-because-the-old-man's-got-the-money-and-you-get-a-degree-razzamatazz-U!' No way! It can't. It's too constipated with admissions and traditions. And no students, relatively speaking. There aren't any students left in those football field lecture rooms taking notes and selling term papers the way we used to as kids. Nope, my boy, that's out. But that doesn't mean the end of the university, not if it can junk a lot of the medieval superstition it's got around its neck, and see the world a little more like General Motors and PBM...then it'll have a new lease on life, relatively speaking. There's millions of non-degree oriented consumers who want to buy everything from hobby-cake-baker-one-shot-specials to professional upgrade and skill development programs...

"No, my friend, the university of the future has other responsibilities. It's got to help people find suitable mates, show them how to invest their money, equip them to read, to sew, to weld, to fly fish, use computers, relatively speaking...

"Education is business, big business, because the world is one big knowledge consumer. But we have to change the packaging of the commodity. In this world, it's the 'box' that counts! People want their puffed wheat in a better box. A box that stimulates. That inspires confidence. The box has got to be good enough to eat! And that's what's got to happen. The next ten years will see the triumphant marriage of the university with the best in private enterprise management system techniques. Tomorrow everybody will be a student. You, Peter my lad. Me. Our grandmothers, relatively speaking...

"But the problem is that if the university is going to be big, really big, business then it's going to have to change radically.

Business means economy and efficiency and profits…getting the maximum output for dollar input. And there isn't a university around that's doing that. This is where PBM and American Synthetics come in. Relatively speaking.

"Where can we help the university cut its costs and make our profits too? There are three main parts to a university's expenses: the physical plant, the faculty, and the administrative superstructure. The plant can be streamlined. Most universities did that with the easy bond money available in the Sixties. The faculty has been replaced by TVs, videotapes, teaching aids, and grading machines which anyone can run. That leaves the 'superstructure', my boy, the 'superstructure'. We've got to arrive at a minimum-maximum cost ratio there too.

"The registrar's office is computerized. Accounting services are rapidly getting there. Public relations can be bought and bottled in New York or San Francisco or London, relatively speaking. No…the big costs left are the high level administrators! You know, presidents, vice presidents, chancellors, provosts, deans, chairmen of faculty…all top salaries, my boy, but no input into the system with any comparable return. Now that doesn't mean that they're not necessary. They lend a certain prestige to a place. Pass out certificates of successful completion. Dish up diplomas. Talk to chambers of commerce. Serve on national and international committees. Visit legislative hearings. And the chamber of commerce or the Rotary won't settle for less than a vice president. Though the garden club will usually buy a dean – especially if somebody in the family knows how to grow azaleas.

"So…how can we help them to cut here, operate on the 'head' without losing the 'heart' of the university, relatively speaking? This is where we get serious, and that's why we've already shown you that PBM loves you and recognizes the value of the bright minds it is acquiring from American Synthetics!

"What you did in Korea and Vietnam was fantastic. Your own statistics show that one out of twenty former GIs probably still has, ah…his inflatable…and there is a growing demand for this American product in the collectors' markets, relatively speaking. We've already reviewed your proposals for going into production again and we've run some of our own independent market surveys.

There seems to be a strong potential in the "playboy" and "playgirl" categories…but the consumer wave of the future, the wave that's in the grade schools, has expressed a strong preference in our surveys for alcohol, drugs, and the 'real thing'. In any case, we'll see what happens…but we want to set a new direction. We want to take a product that was essentially geared to a limited market and develop it in other directions, relatively speaking."

The thought quickly passed behind Peter's varied eyes that PBM was going to propose 'houses full of petroleum product male and female prostitutes' for the campuses. He began doing some quick mileage computations on the various synthetics the lab had available. There wouldn't be the problems with the condoms that they had faced in Korea and Vietnam. These would be college students. The small spark generator could be used to run a fifteen minute recording…programmed introductory courses for first-timers…small talk in a wide range of accents on various intellectual levels…learn while you play courses, a short lecture on Nietzsche and nihilism, catchy tunes (everything from "Girl of My Dreams" to "The Guy Next Door")…and they were far enough along to develop a full line for any and all gender combinations…

However, this wasn't what Gordon intended. "No…that's not PBM's interest. Not that we're against putting money into the entertainment field, if your market studies justify it…but this operation is more serious, relatively speaking…more…more intellectual. Thousands of universities, colleges, normal schools, professional schools are confronted with a dilemma of historic proportions. A growing demand for a cheaper product against skyrocketing salary and fringe benefit costs for upper echelon administrators – chancellors, presidents, vice presidents, deans, acting deans, institute directors, executive officers…

"They've replaced the expensive faculty with videotapes, and installed centralized vacuum systems to suck up the cigarette butts and clean classrooms. The computer does the guidance counseling. In short, relatively speaking, they've taken care of everything but the 'president' and that's what we're going to do!

"The company that gets in on the ground floor today with a good 'presidential product' stands to make the same clean sweep that the textbook boys made in the Fifties and the Sixties before the draft went out and the universities had to replace profs with full-length movies in order to draw any crowds at all. This is where American Synthetics enters in. In short, relatively speaking, we want an 'inflatable administrator'…a 'president' that can be had for under ten thousand, with a ten percent per year maintenance agreement, and a ten percent automatic trade-in after five years (eight years on a vice president, and ten on a dean), regardless of wear or condition. You know, the old 'bring in a broom for a vacuum cleaner gimmick'.

"We want something that can touch 4,000 grads at a commencement, and I mean not just shake their hands, but get right down to the old heart straps with a solid punch-pounding commencement address, you know what I mean…inspire all those kids for life, shake all their hands…and not get a single overheated circuit. And the next day be able to go down to the welding shops where the library used to be and talk to the welders about aluminum seams…and not worry about losing his or her air if a spark goes down a collar…we're not interested in something vague like minds and intellects, we want a product that has heart, lots of heart, that can generate enthusiasm and energy without overheating every time it addresses a crowd. And to make doubly sure, we can install a cooler in its head and a couple of vents in its ears that can handle any amount of pressure and heat that may be put on it.

"You people make the best goddam hair and skin on the market. Take that and put a vent in it someplace where it doesn't show…you used to put 'em in the girls' armpits unless I'm mistaken…I wasn't in Korea, but my boy brought one home, relatively speaking, and that created holy hell when he got married and his wife made him sell it. You know what I mean, motorize it. Install a vent and some hair and one of PBM's 660 mini computer-recorder systems with…say six basic programs…one for the regents, one for the chamber of commerce, one for legislators, a couple for graduates, one for students met crossing the campus, one for Rotary luncheons…let's see…nope…six won't work, but we can take care of that later. And it goes without saying that we're going to need 'em in all gender and racial categories…PBM is an 'equal opportunity supplier' and proud of it! And make 'em all realistic…at least as far as what shows, maybe something a little cheaper inside…not like the war models…nobody's gonna skin one…heh…heh…unless it's the board of regents or supervisors and they oughta know better…relatively speaking…"

Peter liked the idea, detected its genius at once. He could already visualize a secretary inflating a president in a cloak room with an electric bicycle pump while 10,000 seniors, associates, faculty, moms and dads waited tensely for the address that had been carefully worked out and selectively market-tested at both Stanford and Harvard by inflatable deans of faculty.

With PBM's sophisticated electronics systems it would be perfect…and by not installing genitals they could use the extra space for the latest electronic breakthroughs…

"Except maybe the deans of students," said Gordon, "…we're not sure on that one. One of our surveys indicates male students and what's left of the male faculty who run the videos, would prefer a dean who was a little more…ah…human, like you know…seeing him in the john taking a leak like everybody else. Nobody takes a leak with the president or even a vice president…but a dean, he's the guy they all see…relatively speaking. Of course he doesn't have so many speeches so maybe we could cut down on the size of the speakers enough to work in a small drainage system that could be used when the kids get to feeling alienated from the system…relatively speaking."

"Goddammit," was all that Peter could say. They had it figured out. All that was left were the details…which fireproof synthetics…how many different models…what kinds of differences in basics between presidents and vice presidents, Ivy League and state schools…

"Goddammit!"

That was ten years ago. Peter had only been in on the fringe of the Korean and Vietnam things, had taken part in some of the initial research and experiments that American Synthetics had conducted way back then…but he'd catapulted right to the top of PBM/American's top secret 'Operation Academic Excellence'. He had personally discovered the new 'aged' flesh coating that looked a mellow sixty but held its graying fibers like sixteen.

Ann had been with him all the way. Six years ago she'd had Fred – just two weeks and a day after Yale bought its first chancellor and Princeton a director for the Institute of Advanced Studies. Then three years later, as though Ann's labor pains were good luck spasms, on the day Ann Marie was born the State of California system had bought sixteen community college directors, thirty-eight deans, eight chancellors, sixteen presidents, thirty-one vice presidents, eight research institute directors, and a public relations director for the Berkeley campus for sixteen million dollars.

That there wasn't a single campus in the United States that didn't have at least one American Synthetics dean was Peter's personal triumph. And foreign orders, slow at first, were now pouring in from Great Britain, Canada, and the rest of the Commonwealth, spurred in part by Peter's success in gearing accents to purchasers. It was all ample evidence of Peter's skill both as an engineer and as a sales vice president. It was true the Justice Department had made American Synthetics share its know-how. But PBM/American still held the patents and this meant that the competitor, Boston Balloon and Rubber, could only boast a dozen presidents, about three times that many deans, and an academic vice president or two. They were mostly selling heads of departments.

Boards of regents and Trustees councils from coast to coast, and abroad, had placed their absolute trust in PBM/American, and they'd not been disappointed!

There wasn't a single empty classroom in the nation! Not a single idle videotape! The last cost hurdle – 'everything for everybody' – had been cleared out of the way of the golden age of the free university. The advantage of inflatable executives was spreading like chicken pox from universities to government agencies and large corporations. The U.S. State Department had ordered one for one of its key ambassadorial posts. There was even talk in the Republican and Democratic National Committees of purchasing inflatable presidential candidates as a cost-cutting measure. PBM/American Synthetic stocks were priceless and Peter had sheathes of them.

He was also the Company's top troubleshooter as well as vice president in charge of sales. When a year ago an American vice president at Denver University had unstopped the vent on a

Boston Balloon and Rubber dean of graduate studies just prior to the Methodist Women's Alumni Association Dinner in honor of the last retiring faculty member, Peter had been flown in from San Francisco. He had the chancellor back on track and the dean inflated by the time the dessert arrived and in plenty of time for the very moving addresses that each was to give. Of course, there had been mild protest from Boston Balloon, but PBM/American's executive vice president had curtly responded that apparently the quality of Boston Balloon and Rubber's deans of graduate faculty weren't up to American's high academic standards.

Things like this, though, kept Peter busy. Once he had had to fly to Fairbanks, Alaska, where the cold had jammed one of their newer 'auto-inflate' controls on a vice president for Statewide Systems, so that he over-inflated and burst at a Board of Regents' meeting.

More sophisticated equipment meant more possibilities for problems. Peter had spent the greater portion of the last two days at Dartmouth with a director who wouldn't inflate for Rotary. Tomorrow he would be at the University of London with a senior dean who had developed a slow leak. Today, however, he could relax. He was about to be awarded a Doctor of Humane Letters at Poughkeepsie University for his service to higher education. Ann had a cold and couldn't come along, but he had been promised a videotape just for her and the kids.

The sun was a warming spring sun. Crocuses were bursting the grass. He had a couple of hours before the ceremony to walk...just walk...how great it was to walk. He had spent too much time on planes and in taxis in the last months and not enough time just walking. As he strolled along a lilac hedge leafing out, he remembered his own student days. How things had altered since then...

Lost in a mixture of nostalgia and anticipation of things to come, he stumbled over a student dozing on the grass with his head in the hedge out of the sun. He came down hard on the lad's calves with his own knees and sprawled himself flat across a crocus. The fall almost knocked him unconsciousness and it took about thirty seconds to recover enough to be able to focus.

He began to apologize to the lad, who was still stretched out and apparently either dead or very unconcerned. As he stood up, he suddenly noticed the sharp whistling sound of escaping air coming from the prone figure. When he bent over to see if the boy was hurt, it became obvious that the lad was deflating. He quickly pulled the head from the hedge. It was shrinking. As he turned the student over to look at his face, the shirt fell open and he could clearly see the Boston Balloon and Rubber mark on its chest! Boston had beaten them to it!! They already had a test model out! Their products were inferior…but they had a head start this time. That meant they'd be able to assembly line a good six months ahead of American Synthetics…God forbid! The next and greatest round was coming up and it was going to be the hardest. If Boston Balloon and Rubber could have its student models into the stores by fall…my God!

He almost forgot the ceremony. And when the Head of the Board of Governors presented the degree, Peter forgot to stand up and had to be nudged. It didn't even pull him back to himself when the Provost gave the presentation speech that Peter had programmed for him. Across the table sat the Dean of the College of Arts and Sciences, one of American Synthetics' first models…still functioning flawlessly…a man loved by students and administrators alike. For a second a wave of pride swirled around him…followed by an even greater one of despair. PBM/American had won the first round, become a billion dollar corporation. Now it might lose the second round! By fall semester every student that wanted a degree or certificate or a transcript could buy a Boston Balloon and Rubber product and send it off to classes…they wouldn't even know PBM/American existed!

He caught a taxi for the airport as soon as the ceremony was over, the parchment wadded up in his briefcase and forgotten. He was exhausted. Despite his agitation he fell asleep shortly after takeoff. At first all he could see in his dream was the Boston Balloon and Rubber label splashed across the sky of a hideous nightmare, but gradually the sticker faded and Ann's cheerful face smiled out at him from somewhere. The more he relaxed, the more she materialized in his vision…waiting as always there at the front door…the kids too…the electric bicycle pump in her right hand. He smiled in his sleep and stretched against the fastened seat belt.

Passover in the English Department

Prologue

The Indian *Laws of Manu* is most strict and definitive when it comes to the responsibilities of the student, particularly in relation to his teacher. Above all, the student must be diligent and exert himself even without being told to by his teacher, and he should always strive to please his teacher. However, should a student argue with his teacher, dislike him, or criticize him – even if such criticism is justified – the student becomes an ass in the next life. For slandering his teacher he will be reborn a dog. If he dares to 'sponge' upon his teacher, he will be born a worm. And should the student be jealous of his teacher, he will return as a large insect.[1]

Tom Barkman, MFA and instructor of Creative Writing 214, sensed the pending catastrophe in the English Department first. "Poets, as history indisputably establishes, possess a particular perspicacity for detecting the alterations of the karmic winds..." On a Tuesday morning when Tom sat himself at the computer to complete his ecological *Whispers to Accompany the Death of the Environment*, the glowing surface shimmered nonsense...the symbols insignificantly strung across the screen.

A month before, given trends in publishers' interests, he had known he had a great epic poem...now the metaphors had gone slack upon the keyboard. "My God, my God," he wept at the end of four hours, "I've lost my muse!" A week later the muse had not returned. He set searching and discovered all about him a palsied stillness, a "veritable voidness of muses in general."

James R. Roberts, Ph.D., Associate Professor of Communications Skills, at Easter had been certain of a job next year at Ohio State, and escape from "this nest of comma freaks"…so certain that he had built a collage of greater lines from the Dean's worst memos and posted them on the Department bulletin board, entitling the composition "An exercise in the English language as written in our time". Of course, he'd not given the source, but knew that all knew…and it was the sort of thing no grievance committee would hold against him. When Barkman found him, he had just finished the grotesque letter from Ohio: "…the state legislature has cut our budget…our vacancies won't be filled…next year…sorry Jim…Sincerely yours…"

For Roberts it wouldn't be fatal, Tom sensed. Roberts' love of scholarship came to his assistance again just as it had saved him from the draft. He wrote in red upon the collage "An inspiring model for the good student who wants to be better!" He spent several restless minutes wondering if this couldn't be misunderstood, then ended his ill ease with a Xerox copy to the Dean, adding a plea in the name of quality education to be allowed to assist his students in this manner "with some first-rate written communications text!" His carbon paper Nietzsche mustache was limp from the experience for several days, however.

At least two promotions had been anticipated in the Department when the Dean of Faculty, an innocuous man who plumbed one ear with his littler finger when discussing faculty matters, let the Dean of the College know, wiping the nail upon the pants crease where it clove the knee, that there "will be a tightening of lines this year…no advancements that aren't *more* than justified…even a Louisa May Alcott would have trouble here…." The Dean of the College, Doctor of Philosophy in University Administration from Stanford, understood. He and his wife had both been in 'primal scream' therapy for most of the semester and a bold new sense of purpose lighted his ambitions and filled them with images of primal scholars. None of his departments measured up, least of all English, but he would build, build, build!

Perhaps the most tragic instance of all was that of Charles Norman, Ph.D. in Modern English Grammar, who had been working two years on a project in 'modern usage' with a quarter time off from the Department. He had just completed a *Comparative Conjunctional Analysis of the Encyclopedia Britannica* for the 1908 and 1948 editions, in which he clearly established an upward trend in the use of coordinating conjunctions, particularly 'and', 'however', and 'nevertheless', with 112,321 instances of 'and', and 15,004 of 'however,' and 896 of 'nevertheless' in the 1908 edition for a percentage comparison against total coordinating conjunctions of 0.758, 0.100, and 0.005, as opposed to 275,891, 25,206, and 3,529 respectively in the 1948 edition for a percentage comparison against a total of 0.689, 0.063, and 0.008.

He had diagrammed these gracefully and extrapolated a significant 'tendency in 20th century communication trends'. The trend was returned to his desk by the PMLA with a Xerox copy of the same study conducted on the same conjunctions from the same editions done by Professor William Harbon Barber of Perdue. The studies agreed on the 1908 edition down to the last 'nevertheless', but Barber had thirty-seven additional 'and's, twenty-six fewer 'however's, and one additional 'nevertheless' for 1948. The editor was asking both scholars to verify their statistics before he would accept the article on a 'first prove first publish' basis.

"Impossible!" The Department would not extend any more free time...besides he'd ruined his eyes on the first run through. Unfortunately, as Grotes, the Department Head, put it, "Norman, your tenure is tied to a significant contribution to new knowledge."

Grotes, because of a realigning of higher wills, knew he was going to lose the headship; however, the cruel tenure-tie for Norman already existed in a memo to the Dean of Faculty. Norman's wife and blond-headed kids began dedicating their evenings and weekends to the search for a 'significant contribution'.

The casualties accumulated in the next two weeks. Carlton's student rating averages in Elizabethan Drama were down ten points. Alice Baker of Greek and Roman Lit broke a rib when she fell over the typewriter someone had left in the hall outside her office door. The University Senate was toying with dropping the English requirements for the B.A. down to six hours of straight composition, which would probably put most of the Department out of work.

Only Grace Porter, recent Ph.D. in Chaucer, seemed to be having any luck. But in Grace's case, as Bill Williams, Milton '71, pointed out, it might be but a matter of time. "She's got six chapters in her dissertation plus an appendix. She's turned the first five into ten articles and a footnote in Carlson's *Readings in Literary Criticism for Sophomores*. She's got one chapter to go and then it's the appendix…and if she tries that they'll get her for plagiarism."

In an Armageddonic atmosphere the English Department convened its monthly meeting in March. The fear expressed itself in the increased tensions in the battle lines that separated the camps: tenured vs. untenured faculty, communications skills vs. pure scholarship – especially nasty because the former would inherit the earth if the B.A. change went through.

Relishing his last lurch of power as waning Department Head, Grotes pierced the skirmishers with the news that the "State legislature is line-iteming and English is out, my friends…at least three positions." He cool-paced the panic while savoring on the tip of his tongue the bitter taste of the end of his reign.

Fear wriggled up the walls in waves, dripped from the ceiling in steamy droplets that passed through pores of scholars' skins to coagulate upon their backbones and goose ripple their academicians' hides.

"And," Grotes continued, his thin ear lobes, reddened by the moment of truth and his role as its bearer, vibrating softly in time to the darting dance of his Adam's apple…what a fantastic exit, to slay so many former foes with the naked jawbone of job security… "the Dean of Faculty, with the concurrence of the President and the Board, has appointed a committee to determine"…reading now from a crumpled memo retrieved from his jacket pocket…"which departments face significant further reductions in the University's drive to improve quality while streamlining packaging and delivery of our products to the student consumer." The memo re-crumpled itself on the palm of his hand and he returned it to the warm place above his heart. The Adam's apple paused for emphasis. "And the English Department quota, with the changing B.A., will be about fifty-five percent, with affected tenured faculty to be offered commensurate positions in the community college system." The apple pirouetted and gracefully curtsied in place.

A line limped through Barkman's mind. "The sun at noon is a dying sun, our birth is the forenoon of our death." Catchy and significant, but was it original?

Hazelwood – 'The Bible as Literature', 'Hebrew Literature in Translation', and 'Composition 346' – recovered first, rescued by his "I am that I am." A fiery old man whose better fantasies caught him in profile facing pharaoh, holding a sacred serpent rod and scaring the sonofabitch shitless in a series of Cecil B. DeMille night epics, Hazelwood had a sudden day vision. "Why…not…wait…a minute, they can't do that…the sons of Canaan! What happens to scholarship? To academic freedom? What will the students say? Cut the English Department and you've destroyed the University! We'll fight…truth's on our side…on our side…on our side…" Like a broken record, his mouth ran on, but his quick and darting mind had already made an amazing jump. "This is a just and a righteous universe, put together by a just and righteous intelligence, the last appeal in all conflicts. Here was a new occasion for a new Passover…if we just have faith and pure hearts…a lamb…male…and untainted…"

At another time and place his colleagues might have snickered. However, now the future of the University, of scholarship, and quality education were threatened.

Grace Porter – 'Chaucer' and 'Christian Scriptures as an Undergraduate Literary Experience' – whose interest in blood sacrifices grew from a childhood of scratching mosquito bites till they bled in order to sense the funny pain, understood. "But where will we get a lamb?"

Roberts suggested one might buy lamb chops at Safeway and squeeze them into a plastic bag for marking the doors.

Tom wondered if it was the blood that was important, then "…perhaps ground round…a better grade, of course, with less suet?"

"No, no, no!" Hazelwood was adamant. "Not really lambs, no, no! Don't you see? The innocent creatures here are the students…it is all for their sakes…and the sacrifice, the contribution to the future, is theirs! They must be prepared to make it for the sake of the rest of their fellows."

Burton, who taught both 'Freshman Composition' and Sunday School on weekends, grasped the situation now. "Like Abraham and Isaac...the father, for the sake of...of future generations, willing to offer his only begotten student...I mean son!"

Grotes, the atheist, as his Adam's apple suggested even to those meeting him for the first time, had reservations. "But no poor sonofabitch is going to get himself bled willingly. Besides, there's the Dean and the police and the Regents and the body..."

"You're right – there'd be a body!" Grace's experiences with mosquito bites and Chaucer had not equipped her to deal with bodies.

Roberts, on three M.A. committees, suggested one of his candidates. "After all there's a lot more at stake for them...and...they might not be as innocent as freshmen, but there's a certain obligation...we could get them to draw straws and get them to do the...uh...messy part...by promising *two* M.A.s, no strings attached...well...maybe not after all... no that wouldn't work." It had just occurred to him that he would lose a committee assignment, which might make him vulnerable at a poor time. "And there would still be the body," he added with conviction.

Hazelwood no'd again, "No, No! No! We are not criminals, murderers, no, no, no, no, no bodies! Abraham didn't murder Isaac!"

Grace thought that was because the angel arrived on time...wasn't it? She wasn't sure she trusted angels.

"No, no, no, we don't need bodies, only a little innocent blood...from a finger maybe, or an ear lobe...it is not much...a little 'X' on each door, that is all."

"Like vampires almost," encouraged Grace, whose tendency toward the bizarre often upset faculty meetings.

If that were all, Roberts could get it as '...part of the thesis requirement'.

At the end of three hours the Department was agreed, one of only three meetings within memory where this had happened. The student selected was to appear in ten days at a special 'examination by the Department of his thesis'. Roberts nominated a William Jordan, whose thesis the committee members had rejected twice as less than adequate. Not only would Jordan probably be eager to save the future of the humanities in the American university system, his "…ah…intellectual accomplishments are probably more lamb-like than any other graduate in the university." As for the actual puncturing, "Perhaps Jordan himself would be willing….in case…well you know, someone else…not Jordan of course…professional brutality."

"Yes, or bestiality." Grace giggled in anticipation of the coming blood rite. She was going to ask, "Will he have to undress?" but wasn't sure her colleagues would approve. They were not always kind toward her particular view of student-faculty relationships.

Kurtson – 'Biographical Sketches of the Biographers of the 18th Century English Satirists' – was elected to contact Jordan. She wasn't on Jordan's committee and it wouldn't look so much like coercion. Kurtson's interest was considerable for at that moment her proposal for a year's leave and a grant to spend time in Paris on the biographical sketches of the biographers of the 18th century French satirists, was under consideration by the National Endowment for the Humanities.

It was a week before Kurtson located Jordan in a Laundromat on a Saturday. Jordan was doing a year's dirty socks and Kurtson the twin's diapers.

Jordan, before Kurtson could mention thesis and sacrifice, blurted out, "I saw the handwriting on the wall, like, and switched to electronic technology, like, and I'll have the forms on Monday. It's more appropriate to my new career because, like, I'm joining the Navy when I'm done and electronic technology is the thing, like, though I really dig English, like…"

It was too late now. The Department was completely paralyzed by its fear. None of the other graduate students seemed appropriate, "…puffed as it were with too much insight into the Department to really be innocent," as Barkman observed.

Monday morning early when he arrived on campus the Angel of Death was mildly puzzled by the titled doors branded against his coming with tiny 'X's drawn in red ballpoint on University letterhead.

A Miracle with a Moral

Prologue

Two great miracle legends come to us from the lands of the Near East. The first describes the quest for the plant of immortality undertaken by Gilgamesh, the Great Warrior of Sumer, the King of Ur, the Tamer of the wild Enkidu, who became his constant friend and companion. Gilgamesh then entered upon his quest, during which Enkidu was slain for the sins that the pair had committed against the Gods. In his sorrow over the death of Enkidu, Gilgamesh confronted his own mortality. With the help of Urshanabi, the Boatman, he crossed the great sea that separates the living from the dead. And with the aid of Utnapishtim, the immortal man and rescuer of the Gods themselves, Gilgamesh obtained the plant of 'old age becomes youth again', which would render him who consumed it deathless. Carrying the plant back to his city of Ur to share with the elders, he stopped at a cooling pool to wash the dust from his hot and tired body. Suddenly, while Gilgamesh bathed, a serpent emerged from the waters and consumed the precious plant, whereupon it shed its age and old skin. Ah....Gilgamesh, the Great Warrior of Sumer, the King of Ur, the Tamer of wild Enkidu, sat and wept the tears of the mortal.[1]

The second legend relates the miracles that accompanied the travels in Egypt of Joseph, Mary, and Jesus as they fled the fury of King Herod. These are the great but little miracles that serve to illustrate the divine nature of the infant Jesus and the effects of this nature upon all with which his body came in contact. Here they are as we find them in ancient Christian texts. The first is told by a servant girl traveling with Joseph, Mary, and Jesus. In it she describes their encounter with three weeping women:

> I. By them stood a mule, covered with silk, and an
> ebony collar hanging down from his neck, whom they

kissed and were feeding. When she remarked on the beauty of the beast and wondered at their tears, the three maidens, their eyes filled with tears, said that this handsome mule, which she saw now before her, was indeed their brother, born with them of the same mother. They then explained that after the death of their father the three women had done their best to find a suitable bride for their younger brother. Unfortunately, just as it seemed he would marry, a jealous and spiteful witch had turned the young man into a mule. Thus, as they wept they tried to comfort their brother who was now a dumb beast.

When the servant girl heard their story, she urged them to have hope, for a cure for the tragic condition of their young brother was indeed close at hand. To them she explained that she had herself once been leprous, but that her mistress who was the blessed Mother of the divine baby Jesus had sprinkled her sick body with water from the baby's bath, whereupon she had beeen instantly made whole. The three maidens followed her and appealed to blessed St. Mary for her help. And Mary, taking great pity upon them, placed the baby Jesus gently upon the mule's back, whereupon it at once became again the handsome young bridegroom.

(*The First Gospel of the Infancy of Jesus Christ*, Chapter VII)

II. At another time and another place as they traveled in Egypt, there was a mother who brought to Lady St. Mary her ailing son who was on the point of death. Lady St. Mary was washing the baby Jesus and, as the mother pleaded with her to heal her son, St. Mary gave her some of the bath water in which she was washing the baby Jesus and instructed her to sprinkle it upon her sick child. The mother took the water and did as she was told. The child fell into a deep sleep and then after a few minutes awoke healthy and perfectly restored.

(The First Gospel of the Infancy of Jesus Christ, Chapter IX)

III. Once there was a leprous woman who begged of St. Mary that she might heal her of her terrible affliction. Lady St. Mary asked her to wait a while till she had finished washing the baby Jesus and put him to rest. The woman waited as she had been told, and when Lady St. Mary had placed baby Jesus in his bed she gave the woman of his bath water and told her to pour it over her afflicted body. She did so and was instantly made whole.

(The First Gospel of the Infancy of Jesus Christ, Chapter XII)[2]

Have you ever known someone who was born on December twenty-fifth? When one is a child, such a birth date is a great misfortune. There are no parties. Half the day may be spent in church. The annual intake of presents is reduced by fifty percent as thrifty relations kill two gifts with one purchase. When one is older, it does have the advantage that friends and relatives who forget one's birthday still send Christmas cards.

Samuel C. (for Christmas) Peebles, overdue by almost two weeks, was born on Christmas day. His childhood suffering was compounded by a middle name that begged other children to torment him. At all times of the year they would yell, "Hey, Christmas, are you feeling merry yet?" But now he was older, very much older, as his mirror confirmed when he shaved. Most of his business associates and other acquaintances had no idea that he was born on December twenty-fifth or that he even had more than a middle initial. To everyone who had ever visited his apartment on upper 76th he was 'Single Shot Sam'. He liked that. The source of this nickname was reflected in the heads that began in the den and spilled over in glassy stares onto every wall in the apartment, including the bathroom, where hung a musk ox that tended to get moldy. Each of these trophies, from the wildebeest to the leopard, had had its charge, jump, or jaunt terminated by a single shot, with one exception – the great, roar-jawed lion in the living room suspended above the heavy walnut mantel, flanked on the left side by the alabaster ashes of Samuel C. Peebles' first wife, Annie Bell.

"That one," Sam would say, pointing at the lion's head, "he's the one that almost got me! I'd only wounded him, a superficial shot... had a malaria chill at the time, shivering ...unsteady. We followed him down a draw between two scrubby thickets, my mistake that was, because he somehow got behind me while the boys were beating the scrub ahead. Lost my rifle but managed to get my thirty-eight out and...see that tear through the mane on the right side and the hole in his ear...that was my first shot while he was chewing away on my helmet. Taxidermist wanted to fix it up, but I wouldn't let him. I traded that hole in his ear for the piece of mine he chewed off! Well, it took two more belly shots and finally one to the heart to put an end to our wrestling match.

"When we got the side of my head wrapped up and the scratches on my face and arm sort of taped, we skinned the old boy out and found two spear points in his right shoulder and a small slug in the left flank. A tough bugger he was, that he was alright. They say a cat's got nine lives...he'd sure used up eight of his when I finished him off."

Some of the junior members of Peebles, Smith & Linkerowitz insisted that he was called 'Single Shot' for the way he could unerringly bag victory for clients in real estate and divorce cases, estate settlements, and civil suits. But Sam was more than a fearless hunter and attorney, he was also a very religious man who never tired of warning clerks and secretaries of the dangers of sin and sloth. Some of the less respectful younger attorneys repeated among themselves the story that when Sam had first joined the firm he'd specialized in squeezing widows and orphans and that at the end of a squeeze, as a religious man, he had always sent a card offering to make a donation in the widow's name to a charity of her choice, or he would send a bouquet of flowers in season to brighten a hovel before the furniture was repossessed or its residents evicted. Whether these stories are true or only represent the idle gossip of jealous individuals on lower rungs of the ladder of success, I don't know. I have never taken them very seriously. I know for a fact, however, that he was very devout, and if anything, became more so after his second wife, Alice, who was considerably younger, had left him to his trophies and "smelly" cigars after a brief six months. She went off to Key West, as he said, to "squander her mental cruelty money shamelessly in the sun."

His first wife had been considerably older than he and truly a saint. She was the elder daughter of Smith Senior of what was Smith & Linkerowitz and it was she who in marriage elevated the young attorney to partner status and provided a correspondingly appropriate income. They had had no children and, shortly after the death of the elder Smith, Sam's wife, who had always had a heart murmur, joined her father in that law office beyond the pale. Smith Junior replaced his father in the firm. Sam assuaged his sorrows in his passion for hunting. Sometimes when he surveyed his domain and its collection of trophies, he felt like he was a kind of Trophy-Noah saving the best of each species for that great hunting lodge in the sky. Then sometimes, too, he envied these beasts great and small their eternal youth. They never grew older, their eyes, even if glass, were as sharp as ever, their horns and hairs and manes as fresh and vibrant as in that moment at which each had crossed his sights.

Then one morning a sharp pain announced itself without warning in his upper chest. Nothing to worry about, his physician had assured him after a series of tests and checks, a little cramp…but cut back on the coffee, the smoking, get more quiet exercise, take things easy. Maybe it wasn't serious yet, but it certainly seemed to make the figure in the mirror older and grayer and aware that 'the bird of time was on the wing'. Sam was a doer and after a couple of days thinking about it he decided it was time to start doing! If he couldn't do much about his body, he could certainly start doing something for his soul. He had always been a believer, though not a regular participant in any particular brand of religious practice, which he considered both unnecessary and a waste of time if one's heart were in the right place. However, he did start reading the scriptures as he hadn't read them since childhood. As he read, what impressed this Trophy-Noah the most was the veritable smorgasbord of miracles he discovered in the texts. Soon he started to wonder if there might not be some small miracle out there set aside especially for him. At about the same time, he began to sense the significance of the date of his own birth, which perhaps had been intentionally delayed by some greater than human force.

Sam had always believed in miracles…well almost always…there was the day when his faith had been sorely tested in a seventh grade biology class in which the teacher, in expounding upon whales, had made light of the possibility that a man could be swallowed by one of these creatures and then later vomited up whole and undigested on a beach someplace. Sam had expressed his doubt to his father, a Methodist lay preacher who possessed considerable charisma and conviction. As a result, Sam's doubt had been expelled by a sound thwack up side the head with the *King James Version of the Old and New Testaments, Plus Concordance Complete with Multi Colored Maps of Bible Land.* This thwacking had instilled in him for life a firm belief in the power of the Almighty to do whatever he pleased. It was this thought that sent him now to search through the miracles of scripture to see if there weren't one that might be applicable to his condition.

If Abraham at one hundred and Sarah at over ninety could conceive Isaac, couldn't something perhaps at his age be done for him too if he believed? After all, Abraham hadn't really believed at first that he would father a child and must have fallen on his face laughing. And he, Samuel Christmas Peebles, like Daniel, had been in the lion's den, so to speak, and had also survived, albeit with a torn ear and some blood loss. On the other hand, in his case, he had handled the problem himself. It really was a miracle that he'd come out alive…but he had done it on his own without any major expenditure of divine energy…so maybe, just maybe, he had some credit in his account. If Elijah could raise the widow's son at Zaraphath and then travel himself into heaven in a chariot of fire pulled by two fiery horses.... couldn't he expect...just what did he expect?

Well, he had certainly done his part toward earning a little miracle. He had never gambled, had never lied on his tax forms even though there had been disagreements with the IRS over interpretations. He had hated Communism and Nazism and Socialism and the dole and immigrants, and had always been against interracial marriages. He had never engaged in extramarital relations and infidelities during either of his two marriages, nor had he condoned those activities on the part of others. True, he drank socially and had smoked – cigars mostly – at which his first wife had coughed a lot. But after his second wife left him, he had stopped smoking, cold turkey.

As a kid he had thought that being born on December twenty-fifth was a curse. Now that he was getting along in years he suspected that his birth date, coinciding as it did with that Big Birthday, might well have some special significance, might mean that somebody up there was sort of looking after him...and if he could just get his youth back, knowing what he did now about the world, but starting over so to speak, he felt he could maybe really change things, create a new world, do the great deeds one just doesn't always get done in one lifetime. Certainly being made young again would be a miracle. He realized that every year when Christmas day rolled round. His last wife, who'd been gone for several years now, had said he looked a little like a graying Vietnamese pot-bellied pig, but she had been a spiteful you know what, and he was glad he didn't have her ashes in the apartment. If he were young again, he wouldn't need to worry about making money for he had enough and so could concentrate on doing good works. What one needed was faith. When Jesus and his disciples were crossing the stormy sea and the boat began to rock and tip and the disciples were afraid they were going to sink, they awakened Jesus and he calmed the storm, then rebuked them for their lack of faith. There was also the woman who followed him and just reached out and touched his garment and was healed when he said, "Daughter be of good cheer, thy faith hath made thee whole." Sam had lots of faith too! Perhaps he could be made young again?

Many people believe that all the miracles of scripture happened, but that miracles only happen to other folk. This wasn't for Sam. If they could happen – and he believed they could – they could happen to Sam. If whales could be made to swallow unchewed grown men, Sam could be made young again in order to accomplish great things…if he believed…and he believed!

God helps those who help themselves. An old Persian saying, which he'd heard on one of his trips to Iran before the revolution, said: "Trust in God but tie your camel." Trust in God but kill the lion. He was ready to help himself. He had faith – what more could be needed? He studied the scriptures backward and forward and had a Bible constantly open in the apartment and in his office as he searched for signs and hidden meanings.

One day while looking up a term in the Concordance at the local library, he discovered a reprint of Hone's 1820 Apocryphal New Testament that contained those books that were rejected by the Council of Nicea, which Constantine convened in 325 to put an end to the squabbles raging among the bishops in his new state religion. In these books, the *Gospel according to St. Thomas, according to St. Mary, according to St. Peter, and the Infancy Gospels,* he read for the first time of the miracles of Jesus as a baby and young boy – clay figures brought to life, serpent bites cured by simply breathing on them, bridegrooms turned into jackasses and turned back into bridegrooms by having the baby Jesus sit on their backs. Again and again there were references to the miraculous power of the water in which Mary had bathed the infant. Leprosy, cramps, seizures, blindness, visits by dragons – all were healed by application of Jesus' bath water.

On one of the pages in this book he found a handwritten note in the margin next to the story of a leprous woman who had been healed: "It is said that several small Roman glass vials containing drops of this miraculous water still exist." The ink had faded from black to pale brown. It must have been written a long time ago. Probably in the last century. By whom? No matter…if such a Roman vial existed, it was his job to find it. He was born on Christmas day, survived like Daniel the lion's den. He possessed the faith the apostles had lacked on that stormy night…he would go to the holy land to search for such a wondrous flask. He would find his miracle! He would trust in Allah, but tie his own camel.

Peebles, Smith, and Linkerowitz ran on automatic pilot anyway. His presence there as senior partner was more or less pro forma. If miracles didn't come to Sam, Sam would go to the miracles. And go he did. His plan was to fly to Tel Aviv and then on to Jerusalem and from there to Bethlehem and travel as a pilgrim following the trail of Joseph and Mary and the infant Jesus into Egypt.

From a local carpet merchant named Sarki, whose offices were near the offices of Peebles, Smith, and Linkerowitz, and with whom he had had considerable dealings, he secured a letter of introduction to Sarki's second cousin's first son who lived in Jerusalem and traded in antiquities. Sarki himself had come from Jerusalem many years ago, though it was never clear to Sam whether he was Muslim or Jew. In any case Sarki was willing to help.

His second cousin's eldest son was indeed possessor of wondrous things – Sumerian lapis beads, Roman erotic signet rings, early Christian crosses, Egyptian mummy parts, Mohammed's sandals, threads from the saddle blanket that Paul had lost when he fell from his ass on the way to Damascus, Ethiopian masks, quaint little Greek phallus figurines. Upon Sam's arrival, the second cousin's eldest son, reading Sarki's letter of introduction and mistaking Sam's interest in a Roman flask of Jesus' bath water for a commercial interest, not only showed him his display of Roman glass and alabaster vials of bath water, he also took him out back, beyond the 'true cross splinters work room', to the holy bath water division of his enterprise and assured him he could accommodate the American market even during the holiday season for this sacred commodity. He was also, he noted, in a position to supply Mary Magdalen's tears at a greatly reduced wholesale cost and could provide the foreskins of the lesser prophets in various price ranges. At a long counter in one corner of the workroom a young man and an elderly woman were grinding the 'Made in China' labels off the bottoms of small blue flasks. These were then passed on down the counter to be dipped in acid and sandblasted to an iridescent but faded blue by two young women in dusty red headscarves and gray smocks. Finally at the end of the table they were filled with a soapy liquid and sealed with a heavy wax by a couple of boys who couldn't have been much more than ten or twelve.

"But...but..." Sam stammered, "isn't there a real one someplace? The genuine article?"

"Ah." replied the second cousin's first son, who saw a major sale to the American import market slipping away. "Perhaps...there is a story of one such...but...the impossibility, the price, the whereabouts...ah...whereas I can assure you of a constant supply, airmail shipments for the holidays, special reductions for quantities over a thousand..."

In all of his proposal, Sam heard only the word *perhaps*. It was enough, if there was a *perhaps*, perhaps he would find it. He hired a young archeology student with a good linguistics background and headed for Bethlehem. He would follow the scent of that *perhaps*.

As is often the case when one begins to intensely concentrate on an object like a geologic formation, an automobile model, or Roman tear vials, one begins to find them everywhere. These little bottles, which had for centuries been so copiously placed in the graves of everyone from the great to the slightly lesser, were to be found in every market. Some of them were still capped with pitch and glass stoppers. When they came across one so stoppered at a stand or in a shop and inquired as to the contents, they would be assured that it contained Abraham's sweat or some of the darkness God and Moses had cast over Egypt. Once, in a little village between Bethlehem and Al Khalil they were told that the little bottle in the gilded cedar chest contained sacred water. Unfortunately, when the student guide finally succeeded in translating the rest of the faded inscription on the inside lid of the chest, it turned out to be the 'Sacred water of the beloved Immi', the faithful camel that Joshua had ridden to the Battle of Jericho, an ancient and once widely used remedy for baldness and infertility.

Following a rumor to Damascus, they located an elderly scholar who was reported to have an alabaster flask that emitted a golden light and changed the heart and mind of anyone who touched it. This gentleman did indeed possess such a flask, which he was willing to show Sam "as his guest from afar." The flask did shimmer with its own inner light and when Sam was allowed to touch it gently with his forefinger in its muslin wrapped gold encrusted nest, a warm glow spread up his arm and through his whole body. This could only be the sacred bath water of Jesus! When the student had translated Sam's exclamation to his host, the ancient scholar smiled and admonished him with his upraised hand, "It is indeed the sacred water of the bath, but it is of the blessed Prophet of Allah."

After this encounter, Sam was sore depressed. They continued to push southward, pursuing rumors and rumors of rumors, driving over unpaved trails and pathways following a cloud of dust by day and the beam from a single skewed headlight at night. Sam had less and less hope. The miracle he sought, he would not find. Then, lo, as is often the case, when in our seeking we are about to despair, suddenly a door is opened through which the object of our search is glimpsed faintly in the distance.

In a small village between Dimona and Kurnub, near the ruins at Kurnub, they were directed to an old herder who occasionally found pottery fragments and Roman spear points. As they drank tea in his primitive hut, they learned that he did own such a vial that possessed special powers. It had been in his family for more than thirty generations. When his head ached or his wife had difficulty in birthing, he would open the little silver case in which this precious glass rested and the ache or difficulty would immediately cease when one merely gazed upon it!

Sam was allowed to look at the vial and to touch it gently. As he did so he heard a sound as of a baby crying at a great distance, and what seemed like a woman's voice whispering or perhaps humming a lullaby. Although there was no inscription on the silver case in which it lay, there could be no doubt! Would the man be willing to part with it?

"I have many children. To see them go to Tel Aviv to school and become doctors and lawyers and teachers, that is my great wish. I am old and for this I would trade the precious vial which has been in my family for more than thirty generations." An agreement was worked out, funds were transferred from Samuel C. Peebles' share of Peebles, Smith, and Linkerowitz to a scholarship fund in Tel Aviv for the 'sons and daughters of one Isaac Levy'. Samuel Christmas Peebles returned to America with his precious vial wrapped in leather and sewn into the lining of his jacket so that it might not be damaged by the X ray devices at airport security stations.

It was already the end of November by the time he returned to the States. He placed the little flask on a satin cushion on the mantel near the ashes of his beloved Annie Bell, where it could be watched over by the ferocious jaws of the great lion's head. He would decide on that most auspicious day, on his birthday, Christmas day, whether to rub his old body with the fluid or to drink it. Then, like a child dancing around the tree on Christmas morning, he would dance off into youth.

At midnight on Christmas Eve a late-night flight from Poughkeepsie circled over the city, its bright flight lights blinking goodwill and cheer to the city asleep below. Street lamps reflected from an occasional car passing as people left late-night jobs and shepherded their vehicles home to their loved ones. Finally, at heart already an excited child again, he dreamt the best Christmas Eve dream ever!

He was standing in the front ranks of a great auditorium, surrounded by people who were wildly cheering and applauding. Before him on a stage, all parts of which were clearly visible at once, a most amazing performance was taking place. On one side was a marching band in light blue and red uniforms with waving white shakos above radiant faces, each face framed by flowing golden curls. At first he thought it to be a girls' band, but as they turned in a parade maneuver, he could see the great wings that folded on their backs. Above them, row upon row, rose smaller white-robed figures singing Christmas carols. On the other side of the stage were dozens of mules lined up next to one another facing the audience. As he watched, a small infant was set upon the diamond-studded saddle blanket of each animal and it instantly became a handsome, dark haired young man. And each young man resembled every other. Suddenly he recognized them…they all had Sam's face, that is, Sam's face the way it had appeared in the class photo taken his last year in law school, under which the caption had read "most likely candidate for the Supreme Court." In the center of the stage, presiding over and directing this mass of parading angels and transforming mules, flanked on the right by an adoring Annie Bell and on the left by a glowering, teeth-gnashing Alice, stood Samuel Christmas Peebles as he had appeared in the newspapers when he'd won his first Coal Mine Owners wrestling match against John L. Lewis and his scruffy band of miners. This young vision of himself seemed to be saying something, but it was lost in the tumult. Above its head a great flock of doves were circling, carrying balloons upon which was written "he's the one!"

In the wonderful chaos of the marching angels, the applause, the transforming mules, the very hall itself began to sway…or it could have been a slight earth tremor that softly rocked the cradle of the sleeping city so gently that it was no more than a passing subway train, certainly not enough to awaken anyone or to cause a passerby to more than wonder whether he had sensed it or not, just enough to loosen the aging hooks that held the lion head over the mantelpiece. It descended with a crash that echoed through the apartment and erupted onto his dream stage. Blinking and still dazed, he lighted the living room and saw the great head fallen low to the floor, its ninth life, released at last, ascending from its slowly closing eyes. Shattered blue fragments mixed with ash glistened in its shaggy mane like sparkles on a Christmas wreath.

That day Samuel sat down, weeping.

Over his face the tears flowed.

MORAL: The moral of this story is that one should not place much store in old Persian sayings.

The Man Who Worked at Crunchy's

Prologue

At least three ways of looking at old age come to us from the ancient classics of Eastern and Western philosophy. Democritus of Abdera (450-370 BCE), the father of Greek atomism who lived to be 109, lamented that old age was a form of physical mutilation in which the body still possessed its various parts, but each of them was afflicted with some sort of deficiency. [1]

Confucius (551-479 BCE), on the other hand, rejoiced in the self-control and freedom that long life provided him. As he looked back over his lifetime he could say that when he was fifteen he concentrated upon learning and knowing, by the time he was thirty his character had been formed, at forty he had achieved understanding beyond ambiguity, at fifty he understood the Mandate of Heaven and the order in society and nature, at sixty he was at peace with what he heard around him and by seventy he could follow his desires without violating moral principles.[2]

A third approach to old age was offered in the Hindu *Laws of Manu*, which suggests that when a man (the head of the family or 'householder') notices the 'wrinkling of his skin', the 'graying on the top of his head', and finds that he is trying to live in a house full of grandchildren, it is time to leave for the forest and give up the foods and comforts of home. He is to live the life of the ascetic, sleeping under trees and eating only the simplest of foods. If he has a wife, she may either accompany him or stay behind to be cared for by her sons.[3]

In early January, the Tuesday morning edition of the *Telegraph* informed the breakfasting community that in their midst CRUNCHY'S SUPERMARKET employed the OLDEST BAG BOY IN THE UNITED STATES OF AMERICA! People he had never met recognized him from his photo and greeted him on the street. Women at Crunchy's waited in line to have this stooped and ancient bagger tote their purchases, and helped him with the cans and heavier cartons, a thing no one certainly did before the *Telegraph* discovered this eighty-five year old retired railroad conductor who had 'gone back to work'.

Baldy Crunchy had hired him because he reminded him of his own father. And it was Baldy Crunchy who put the *Telegraph* onto the possibility of a good story. It worked. People came to see the old baggy and bought things they didn't need just to have him carry them out – lighter luxuries, cream pies, custards, snails.

This classic box boy, fueled on cheaper ports from Crunchy's Bottle Box at special rates for the help, scootered ice cream and canapés between electric eyes into the parking lot, showing off – his style showing up the more conservative kids in ties and pimples who were too young to enter the BOX. In a land that has never tipped its baggers, people began tipping this antique baggy – generously. They were only mildly annoyed when he dropped their sacks or let his winter nose drip into their purchases.

His face, cracked with age, was like a misglazed pot where ancient blood vessels like stains of inexpensive port crinkled about his nose in little red canals that fed the scattered, leafless mustache hairs growing there, frosty in the cold or sagging in summer heat. Other such vegetation sprouted in profusion from his ear holes as though someone had stuffed his head with dry grass to build a fire, but hadn't been able to locate a match to light it.

Bushy gray arches capped his eyes and set them deeper than they really were, accentuating their cataracted glance, especially in the rear of the store where Crunchy used incandescent bulbs over the vegetables instead of fluorescent because, as Crunchy said, "Fluorescents makes them vegetables too sick lookin', like pukey blue parsnips…no woman in her right mind's gonna buy pukey blue parsnips."

The old baggy's favorite section of the market was the stall of glassed dreams that awaited him behind the Western-style swinging doors of the Bottle Box. After a trip there the trains ran on time in his head, his old ticket puncher clacked a two-step on top of the dresser, and Queen Victoria, whose ticket he'd never punched, but whose ticket he'd often dreamed he might, appeared in white-laced hands and naked fingertips, proffering graciously her tiny slip…

The deep, sweet red in the bottles called to the sweet red in his veins, sparkled through the doors, asked him to dance, to share his check or tips. Before Crunchy had hired him, he'd hardly had enough to feed himself and buy a small bottle now and then on his railroad pension. Now that he could do more for his friend trapped there in the glass, how could he refuse?

He wasn't an alcoholic of the usual sort. During the week he was careful to take only three or four glasses of an evening, sometimes one in the morning if it were cold or raining. He saved his heavy drinking for the lonely weekends. At one time he had brought a preserve jar with his lunch, but this had caused difficulties and he'd had to stop. Crunchy didn't arrive at the Second Avenue market until after noon. He spent his mornings at the Main Street place. He never noticed if his elder baggy was woozy in the mornings, but afternoons he was there and could smell the lunch break and observe its effects in the way the carts wove.

The first time Crunchy had cautioned. The next three times he had fired him, and each time after Crunchy'd relaxed and reconsidered, remembered his own father who had drunk a healthy portion, he'd relented. The last time, however, he made it clear that he regretted that he'd relented. "Goddammit, I'm soft like an eggplant that's been squeezed all week by crazy housewives…yep, that's it, I'm soft. Well, I'm not gonna be soft no more. Nope, no more rotten eggplant in there for a heart! From now on it's all steel and canned tomatoes. Just one more time, you soggy old bastard, and you've had it! Hear me, had it!" There was a kind of firmness in it that convinced. He left the preserve jar at home.

About this time Crunchy got the idea for the *Telegraph*. The reporter came. "How old are you gramps? What'd you do before you bagged? Railroad pension…Social Security…

married...dead...how long...relatives...do you still think about it...pinch the checkers, ha ha...ambition...how do you like the work...bags too heavy...know anybody else your age who bags?"

He had seen Baldy Crunchy talking with the guy behind the office's glass partition. When the reporter identified himself and assured him he wasn't from the pension people, the baggy figured Crunchy was fixing to sell more eggplant. He didn't expect what happened and when it happened, it almost overwhelmed him.

The checkers started calling him grampa instead of boy. Mrs. March in the Bottle Box extended him credit. He bought ten extra copies of the *Telegraph* and sent them to his daughter, Margaret, who lived in Kankakee. She wrote a brief note about "how nice it all was", and something about "old people who keep busy and aren't burdens..." He'd once written her that he might move to Kankakee to be near her as his only surviving relation. But either the letter had gone lost or she'd forgotten to answer it.

His dreams promoted him from third conductor to supervisor. Baldy Crunchy began calling him grampa too, and gave him a twelve cent increase to show how proud he was that the oldest baggy in the United States of America worked in his store.

The Chamber of Commerce presented him with a plastic plaque. The Lincoln Memorial Historical Society had him speak to a luncheon meeting on the golden years of American railroading.

By the first of May, however, the excitement had died down and the world gradually mislaid the fact that the oldest baggy in the United States of America worked at Crunchy's Second Avenue store. Women didn't seek out his line or help him with the heavier bags. They began to complain again that he was too slow. The tips ceased as suddenly as they had begun.

At about the same time a nasty bout of the screws moved into his backbone and set up housekeeping among his dried and frozen discs. He slept with his legs up to his chin and a hot water bottle plastered to the middle of his spine. His walk was a lower primate shuffle that bent him into the wind.

The younger baggies avenged themselves now for the tips and the publicity. When they carried out their loads behind him, they imitated his limp. The customers complained ever more loudly at his slowness. He dropped the plaque dusting it, and it broke. The one person who remembered was Mrs. March in the Bottle Box who continued to extend credit and cut his accounts back from her own pocket at the end of the month.

Only when the tracks were thickly oiled did the trains run on time and the screws neglect their domestic squabbles. Again Crunchy caught him with the preserve jar. He didn't fire him, but he took back the twelve cents and set him to sweeping floors.

Sweeping was better for his physical state because at least he could lean on the broom when the screws got to quarreling, but he was back to third conductor No...less than that...he was a mucker in his dreams cleaning out boxcars.

Some days the lumbago hunched him so he could only pull the broom around. If it hadn't been for Mrs. March's kindnesses he wouldn't have made it past noon. Crunchy didn't seem to care now whether he drank or not, possibly because the broom required less maneuvering skill than the carts.

When the spring days warmed into summer he could unbend a little but he still needed the preserve jar for lunch. By early summer he was almost completely blind in his right eye. The cataract sealed that side of him into his head where only a light-dark distinction existed. The left eye irrigated the gray stubble on his left cheek with a constant flow of salt water, but he could still see clearly if he closed his lids and wiped them out with his sleeve.

In the fall he made his great discovery – he could change people's appearances by changing the way he looked at them! This is a secret that every child knows and then forgets. He must have known it too, long, long ago, but he too had forgotten. If he squinted his watery eye one way, the lids compressed people horizontally. When he opened the eye as wide as it would go, it stretched people vertically. By opening his eye wide and then quickly squinting, the sudden pressure on individuals caused them to puff out at their weak points like old inner tubes. With women it was almost always either the breasts or the ass ends that gave. With men it was likely to be the cheeks or noses or bellies. Thinner customers tended to blow at the knees or elbows while their bodies went wiry as pipe cleaners. Sometimes the heads would take the full blast and the poor bastards would almost float away! The damndest part of it all was that they stayed that way even after he'd closed his eye and cleaned away the waterfall. It was funny how other people around him tried to ignore the bizarre transmogrifications. Often, even the people he'd changed pretended not to notice anything. This made them even funnier with their clothes popping at the seams, with bloated chests, bellies, and bottoms, while their little pinheads tried mightily to look as if the only thing that concerned them in that awful condition was the price of eggs or avocados. Most times though, the person he had worked over gave him a startled stare and moved quickly to some other part of the store.

When his creations became too incongruous, he couldn't suppress his laughter and had to hold onto the broom handle to keep from shaking so hard that the screws would twist him all to hell.

Then, by Jesus, he almost couldn't believe it himself the first time he saw one, when these balloons came back into the store a week later it was the same scrunched and scraunched way they'd left, still trying to let on like they didn't notice! He really fixed them then! If they were puffed he stretched them, and if they were stretched he shrunk them – pressed his eyeball hard with his forefinger so they went lopsided as well! Or erased their hair by pulling his upper lid down in such a way that everything above their ears vanished. He kept this one especially for people who looked too self-important the second time around. In all fairness, he never erased a part of anybody the first time…only if, when they came back, he figured they'd not learned a damned thing.

His failing eyesight made it possible to tip and tilt and convex and concave in ways he'd not have otherwise been able. He flattened the pimply box boys, but he didn't bother the checkers, they'd never done him harm. Nor did he change Mrs. March of the Bottle Box. In fact he almost confided to her once that he was responsible for the grotesque that was picking up a six-pack at the cooler, a middle-aged man twisted into an all-day sucker, upper torso a great round ball, but from the belly downwards a thin split spindle no more than a finger wide. He'd controlled the width carefully on this one by using his fingers like an open rifle sight, shutting the eye gap till just a sliver had slipped through, letting everything puff out the top. He didn't tell Mrs. March. He wasn't sure she would not get word back to Crunchy as to who was messing up his customers.

That trick with his fingers was a good one. He could turn people into flyspecks by looking at them through his fingers formed into a tube, or through a hollow wrapping paper roll. The display counters and shelves, he now discovered, were full of props. Squinting at some bald guy over a whisk broom gave him a straw thatch that wouldn't stop. Under an inverted light bulb he achieved the opposite effect on people with lots of hair.

He was so busy he almost forgot to sweep the floors and dust the canned goods. Crunchy talked to him about this a couple of times, but he didn't mention the things he did to people so apparently he didn't know who was responsible. As Crunchy walked away he was tempted to squint his backside up. That might be going too far...besides Crunchy'd been good to him.

The more possibilities he exploited on the shelves for altering the customers, the more postures he developed for doing so. One woman in furs, through a separated salad dressing with his eye half shut, head to one side, was so wild he couldn't help himself and laughed till he had to take the afternoon off to lie with his knees hunched against his chest and the water bottle on his back. The screws got him so bad it took thirty minutes just to change the water in the bottle. The worst of it was every time he thought about that puffy pile of bosom in its fur trim all done up in orange salad dressing he had to laugh again. After this experience he worked up to his more dramatic effects gradually, taking just bits and pieces, like legs squinted between the cornflakes boxes from the next aisle. He bowed them in or out, or puffed a calf with what he called the watermelon effect, then strolled to the end of the aisle to watch the owner hobbling along.

Of course it didn't seem to hurt anybody physically, not like the screws anyway. He didn't really want to do that, hurt anybody, just overhaul the stuck-ups. Once, he'd managed to restore her youth to an old lady by winking at her through the plastic wrapping and the holes of a chunk of Swiss cheese. She blossomed, lost her wrinkles and her stoop...probably due to the moisture on the inside of the package. When he cleared the water from his eyes and looked at her normally he was amazed! She must have been too for she smiled a kindly thanks in his direction for what he'd done. He tried several times after that to help people that he thought really needed help. Sometimes it worked, sometimes it didn't.

They began to pay more attention to him – particularly those individuals who'd been overhauled several times. They complained to Crunchy that they didn't like the way the ex-baggy peered at them through the glassed carrots and the vegetable oil jars. They called him a nut. That was how they tried to get even for what he'd done to them. One day Crunchy caught him lodged among the dog food sacks watching women's knees – or God knows what – through a glass of chicken noodle soup. Crunchy grabbed him and yanked him out of there in a hurry. It had taken him five minutes to get into the position. Crunchy had him out in five seconds! The screws really let him know about it. They took up where Crunchy left off. He didn't do that one again, though he had begun to achieve some very gratifying effects through the noodles. Crunchy would fire him for sure. Besides, the screws said "NO!"

By the end of October, with the summer tourists gone, there were almost no originals left. Everybody who came into Crunchy's Second Avenue store displayed his handiwork. Some of them he had transformed so often through various juices and half-squints that he had completely forgotten how they first looked. The only originals were Mrs. March, the checkers, Crunchy, and the guy who squirted the vegetables.

By the middle of December, to relieve the monotony, and to celebrate the Christmas season, he started color scheming, running everyone through bottles of maraschino cherries. He was just switching to green with Mrs. Gordon, wife of the President of the First National Bank, when Crunchy caught him and fired him in front of her…knocking the maraschino cherries onto the floor where the bottle broke and ran green blood over their shoes.

Crunchy pulled and pushed the old ex-baggy up to the office, banged the glass door open, glared into his ledger and paid him out to the end of December. Then he dragged him to the front door, triggered the electric eye with his foot. Outside, the baggy stumbled against a cart and almost lost his balance. He paused to dust his pants, bent down as best he could and with his hanky wiped the juice off his shoes. As he straightened up, he glanced through the window. Baldy Crunchy was talking to one of the checkers with his back toward the front of the store.

Crunchy didn't know it, but he'd just lost his insurance. The old baggy put his tongue to the cold glass and produced a great puddle of saliva. Then, pushing his nose where his tongue had been and squeezing his left eyeball this way and that, he went to work on his one-time benefactor. Slowly the shiny bald spot began to expand like a pot on a wheel. Vertically, then horizontally, larger, longer, until the bald spot and Crunchy were one and the same – a huge flesh balloon edged in a graying fringe. Fantastic!

As he stared at his work of art, a sudden tear, or perhaps it was a postnasal drip that had lost its way, crowded into his good eye. He hesitated a moment, then, holding the fleshy bubble steady with his compressed eye and pushing his nose inward on the glass as far as he could with the other hand so that it pointed right at the middle of that field of glassy pink, he very carefully spelled out "I Quit Anyway" on the glass, through the glass, upon the skin dirigible that Crunchy had become. Done, he stood back, closed his smarting eye and wiped it clean with his maraschino-scented handkerchief.

Then the oldest baggy in the United States of America took his screws and hobbled off to the Trailways Bus Depot to hunch his back against the steam radiator that puffed away there on the north wall. It was there that Crunchy found him…hard asleep…hearing whistles again of trains that had so long been stilled.

Job Remembered

Prologue

The book of *Job* in the Hebrew Scriptures tells that once upon a time...

"There was a man in the land of Uz, whose name was Job; and that man was perfect and upright, and one that feared God, and turned away from evil."

(Job 1:1)

"Now it came to pass on the day when the sons of God came to present themselves before Jehovah, that Satan also came among them. And Jehovah said unto Satan, whence comest thou? Then Satan answered Jehovah, and said, From going to and fro in the earth, and from walking up and down in it. And Jehovah said unto Satan, Hast thou considered my servant Job? For there is none like him in the earth, a perfect and upright man, one that feareth God, and turneth away from evil. Then Satan answered Jehovah, and said, Doth Job fear God for nought? Hast not thou made a hedge about him, and about his house, and about all that he hath, on every side? Thou hast blessed the work of his hands, and his substance is increased in the land. But put forth thy hand now, and touch all that he hath, and he will renounce thee to thy face. And Jehovah said unto Satan, Behold, all that he hath is in thy power; only upon himself put not forth thy hand. So Satan went forth from the presence of Jehovah."

(Job 1:6-12)

Having been about and around together since before the start of time, they had become accustomed to one another, perhaps even fond of one another in the way one can become attached to a habit. And it came to pass that once every millennium or so they would meet someplace to reminisce and compare notes on the nature of things. For both of them those meetings offered a chance to relax, leave the concerns of office behind, and escape the droning of hosannas or the incessant whining over lack of air conditioning.

The locations of those encounters were loosely set, though out of professional courtesy and consideration for one another, they usually occurred on earth, sometimes on a mountain peak or in a forest glen. Such places were not really Satan's style, who had little use for scenic wonders and for whom a touch of arthritis had developed in his left elbow some twenty thousand years ago, which acted up at meetings on mountaintops and in cumulus clouds. He, being the more social and sociable of the pair, preferred the chaos and clang of great cities. This time, since it was his turn to name the spot, he had selected Belize City with its fermenting crowds and steaming hot beaches of the South Atlantic. He normally spent a lot of time here anyway, for he had a number of clients scattered around South America who could be easily reached from Belize. In addition, the local blend of prostitutes, car thieves, drug dealers, smugglers, politicians, and gamblers always made him feel at home.

It must be said, however, that the Almighty was a little less enamored of the choice. "A sleazy place...too many people, too much noise...and look over there, what are they doing under that beach umbrella?"

"Ah, that's the problem with omni-vision – you don't really want to know what they're doing."

"Why, that's unnatural! I certainly didn't fashion them to do that!"

"Oh, they're inventive little devils, if you'll pardon the pun. Chalk it up to the tropical heat – they don't do it under beach umbrellas in the Arctic. Just ignore them."

Apart from scenes of this sort, Belize City was an ideal spot. The locals took both of them for American tourists, one of whom could have used a lot more sun and the other who'd had too much. Satan had brought with him a splendid two-hundred-year-old French cognac he had gotten from a Dominican monastery on his way through France, and they inhaled its delicious aroma, sampled its mellow tang, relaxed, and settled back to enjoy the moment...

Ah!" the Almighty sighed. "The centuries seem to go so quickly..."

"Indeed," agreed Satan, "and I would be the first to admit that your creation of human beings has provided a wonderful way to pass cosmic time, although most of us advised against them back then." And he proposed a toast to this marvelous invention as he refilled their glasses.

"Yes," admitted the Almighty. "But there have been moments when I thought they were going to self-destruct. Sometimes I wonder if they don't take their brief performances too seriously."

"That, dear colleague, comes from giving them 'free will'. Of course it's made their activities the more intriguing for me, but, as most of us suggested before you did it, it has proven to be an endless source of disappointment for you. It might have been better to have left off with musk oxen and water buffalo. Really, I can't complain, for in exercising their free will they do tend to mostly choose evil, and to do so gladly and for the most part they remain steadfast in the path they have selected. By the way, speaking of paths, have you in your wanderings encountered my faithful servant evil Orville? Now there's a lad who from childhood on has singularly and wholeheartedly dedicated himself to evil. Oh certainly he did all the little things the wicked as wee ones do, lying, cheating, talking back to their parents and teachers, stealing, relieving themselves in the sandboxes on nursery school playgrounds. But even as a child, Orville was unique. In fact, the limp that marks his gait today was acquired as a toddler because wherever he toddled, he would stretch and strain his wicked little legs in order to step on all the cracks in the sidewalks, for he had once heard other children chanting, 'Step on a crack, break your mother's back.' Such a sense of commitment and dedication has always been rare. Today it is practically nonexistent."

"It reminds me," mused the Almighty, "of my servant Job and our little contest so long ago, which as you recall I won."

"But only after you'd flustered and blustered at him about Leviathan and your might and majesty and your ability to call down the lightning to fry him. Now evil Orville, he's got backbone – he wouldn't knuckle under to blustering like that. Let's face it. Job just wasn't a fair test of commitment."

"Alright," said the Almighty. "Why don't we see of what stuff your servant Orville is made. I'll wager I can get him to abandon you once he's really tempted to do good and exposed to the terrible wages of wickedness."

"Ha," laughed Satan. "If you think you can either scare him or tempt him, you're wrong, wrong, wrong – most of his friends have been indicted. He has one son who is a Mormon missionary, another who is a Catholic priest, and his third wife, after the divorce took up playing in a Salvation Army band. Orville has seen good and bad in all their forms. And in his trials and temptations he has remained steadfast in his commitment to sin. But if you think that in your bag of tricks you have something that would cause him to abandon the way, go ahead and try it. Only one condition I would place on your efforts – you're not to smite him. You have a nasty way with your smites and don't understand your own strength. But 'temptation', fine, go ahead, tempt him with all the goodness you can muster. And let evil Orville's soul go as prize to the winner."

They sealed the bargain with topped up glasses of Dominican cognac and agreed to check with one another from time to time to see how the contest was progressing.

Back in paradise, the Almighty called a council of the saints and greater angels to explain the wager to them and seek their advice. St. Torquemada suggested that if he could only spend a couple of days interviewing the client at his old place in Seville, he would have what was left of him just begging to do good deeds.

"No," said the Almighty. "The agreement was that he has to abandon Satan and choose to do good of his own free will."

"But," objected St. Augustine, "I've always found this free will business exaggerated. Let's face it. Man is like a horse and either your Worship or his Wickedness sits on his back, so he's never without a rider."

"We agree," said St. Skinner and St. Pavlov with one voice. "There's nothing like carrots and cattle prods to make human beings do what they want and want what they do."

"No, again," said the Almighty. "It has to be a matter of his free choice and his free will. We can tempt him with goodness, but we can't force him to take it. He must of his own volition see the goodness of good and the badness of bad."

"Well," urged St. Anthony, who was pretty much the resident specialist on temptation, "let's give it a try. I think the best approach would be to turn his attention inward, inspire him to introspect, get him to self-analyze, to reflect upon the wanton wickedness of his ways, to meditate upon the great mystery of being. For example, the Buddha Sakyamuni abandoned a life of pleasure and ease when he encountered the four states of the human condition."

Anthony's proposal was approved and four of the lesser angels were dispatched to earth disguised as a sick man, an old man, a dead man, and a monk. Over the next few weeks, they managed to cross Orville's path near his law offices in downtown Poughkeepsie. Unfortunately, the attempt to induce insightful self-reflection met with mixed results. For example, Orville tried in the case of the dead man to contact his beneficiaries and institute a malpractice suit against the attending physician and the hospital, asking only for eighty-five percent of any eventual award. Then a mortuary in which Orville was a silent partner tried to sell the dead man's loved ones a twenty-five thousand dollar gold-plated entry visa to eternity. To the old man he suggested that the fair distribution of his estate could only be guaranteed if Orville's firm were made its executor. The sick man was enrolled in an HMO for which Orville's firm fended off the lawsuits of the disgruntled. The monk was promised a sizeable charitable donation to his religious order if he could convince his bishop that the fields owned by the order in upstate New York would make an ideal place for an international toxic waste dump.

Shortly after this attempt at insight Satan stopped by on his way to a religious war to chide the Almighty upon his lack of success. "Are you ready to give up?"

"No way. That was just a trial – and since Buddhists tend to be atheists, I was skeptical of the plan from the outset. No, it is clear at this point that evil Orville just isn't into introspection. But I'm now ready to get serious!"

"OK, you can try again…but no smiting. Remember our agreement. Your minions are not to touch a hair on his head. I don't want to collect a soul at the end that has been snatched bald-headed in processing."

"No problem, we will use analogies, metaphors, allegories, and the indictments of all his colleagues at the firm on charges of extortion, perjury, tax evasion, bribery, and check kiting."

"Fine, but remember members of my staff will be watching members of yours."

Thus it came to pass – senior partners, junior partners, wives, sons, daughters of partners, and the cleaning lady and her common-law husband and companion of many years were not only indicted, they were also sentenced to extended terms in inhospitable prisons. In their preparations for the trials, no one noticed that the DA, prosecutors, and chief investigators were being ably aided and assisted by heavenly hosts disguised as finks, stoolies, FBI agents, CIA operatives, ATFA officers, and various witnesses who were able to produce records long assumed burned and shredded, thanks to the divine policy of keeping track of everything from dropping sparrows to falling hairs and making copies of all shredded documents that might be useful later in establishing admissions qualifications for applicants to paradise. It has since been suggested that it was one of those heavenly emissaries who appeared in a dream one night to Richard Nixon and suggested he too should tape all of his meetings for the sake of posterity.

However, just as the trap was about to close on evil Orville himself, the judge presiding over the whole affair suffered a heart attack that removed him from the bench indefinitely and his replacement happened to be, if not an old friend, at least the owner of a more sympathetic ear who let Orville plead guilty to the lesser charge of parking in a loading zone and permitted him to turn state's evidence and testify as an insider to the iniquities of his colleagues.

Unfortunately the various sums of money the firm's members were accused of misappropriating were not recovered, although rumor hinted that Orville knew in which Swiss bank they had been deposited. Of course, these rumors could have been set in motion by disgruntled heavenly hosts, as Satan insisted. But then, as the Almighty suggested, Satan had played a less than honorable part in the heart attack when one night a week before the trial was set to begin one of the more humongous and hideous inhabitants of hell had made a bare-ass naked courtesy call on the judge. In any case, evil Orville paid his parking ticket and left the proceedings for his winter home in Florida, more convinced than ever that bad is good and good is bad.

The next time Satan and the Almighty met and discussed the matter, there was noticeable tension in the air, which not even two-hundred-year-old Dominican cognac could assuage. Though they remained civil, each clearly felt that the other had played less than fair. But, as colleagues of very long standing, they decided that the Almighty could have another shot at evil Orville.

This time it was decided to approach Orville through his friends and acquaintances who could argue from personal experience on the wages of wickedness and the benefits of goodness. The first choice was Paul Smith, one of his former partners, in whose office Orville had frequently schemed nefarious schemes.

Smith had been a promising, if naive, young law school graduate who had taken the bar exams while working for the firm. Upon their successful completion he had been promoted to junior associate and – given certain inducements – made the fall guy for the firm in a gambling and bribery scandal. That had been several years ago and, because of his age, clean record, and lack of insight into and information on the firm, the courts had been lenient. He received five years, served two, found God, was released, and started his own promising radio evangelical hour. He proved quite charismatic in his 'pulpit of the airwaves' and donations flowed in, which he used to support orphanages and homes for aging widows.

Then one night he dreamt that he personally had been called to facilitate the rescue of the soul of his old associate, Orville. He visited him in Orville's office, talked about the wages of sin and the uplifting rewards of charity, and shared his dreams for starting his own TV program. Orville listened to him, listened to several of his radio programs, looked at his financial ledgers, and was convinced. He bought the station, complete with the 'pulpit of the airwaves', which he rebaptized 'the pulpit in the clouds' and turned into a TV broadcast, interested a national network in running it, and increased donations by a solid one thousand percent within six months. He took forty-seven percent of gross revenues for his own costs and sold the whole lot to an expanding religious network a year later at a considerable profit, which he invested in a company paying starvation wages to widows and orphans making basketball shoes in a bankrupt Third World country, thereby generating an eighty percent annual return on investment. Orville had clearly demonstrated at least that religion pays, even if goodness doesn't.

The second assault upon his errant ways was entrusted to an IRS agent who had worked on the investigation of Orville's law firm and who had been responsible for putting everybody but Orville away. This was, however, no normal IRS agent. He was a man of sterling silver character who constantly put in uncompensated over-time, took no sick leave, and who not only paid his own income taxes punctually, he also routinely overpaid them by ten percent as his tithe to the welfare of the United States of America, one nation under God, indivisible, with liberty and justice for all. He could not be bribed or intimidated.

Once he was put on Orville's case he spent endless uncompensated overtime hours trying to convince Orville that it would be to his advantage as a citizen and patriot to give up all the ill-gotten gains that rumor said he kept in a Swiss bank. Orville at first denied it and then, because the agent persisted, dared him to find it if he thought it existed. This, with a little supernatural aid, is indeed what happened, and this time the courts weren't so lenient. The Swiss deported the cash. Then the widows and orphans in his shoe factories either starved to death or went to work for a competitor for two cents a day more. Vandals slashed the tires on his new Mercedes, his Florida estate was confiscated in a marijuana raid, his fourth wife sued him for back alimony payments, and his fifth wife found the quickie Mexican divorce was illegal and came home to pick up nagging in mid-sentence where she had last left off.

"Surely," thought the saints and the angels, "Orville must now be relenting, softening, realizing that iniquity does not pay after all." But just to be sure, they proposed to launch one final assault on his conscience. This time the Archangel Percival, who was almost a head and a half taller than most of his colleagues and tended to stand out in the heavenly chorus line, was to be disguised as a little match girl selling Girl Scout cookies door to door on a cold winter's eve just three days before Christmas, when the spirit of giving had thickened the very air itself. If Orville bought a box the Almighty would win and evil Orville's soul would be saved. The difficulty with the plan seemed to be mostly persuading Percy, who was a very proud archangel, to squeeze into the little match girl costume and push Girl Scout cookies door to door.

Thus it came to pass that, as the millennium drew to a close and the Almighty and Satan met for a last time in its shadow, they opened the last bottle of Dominican cognac and prepared to toast that outcome of which each was so certain. All the while Percy was moving house by house and apartment by apartment closer to his goal. Unfortunately, the little match girl costume was much too tight in the shoulders with his wings tucked in and gave him a quasi Quasimodo look. And the Girl Scout regulation shoes were too small for his feet, which were large even for an archangel. Still, he limped and bravely hobbled as he marched toward his goal.

The cognac was open, the glasses filled, both waiting expectantly for the report…suddenly Percy, disheveled, broken matches hanging in his hair, cookie crumbs in his feathers, and smelling like cheap peppermint, stumbled across the beach, tipping over umbrellas as he came.

"The dirty bastard…"

"Wicked bastard," corrected Satan.

Percy paid no attention. "He…he…"

"Yes, get control of yourself Percival," growled the Almighty.

"He said he would buy the cookies, but wanted to try a sample to be absolutely sure. I gave him the box and he ate half of them and then gave the rest back, saying they were stale and besides he didn't like mint flavor. When I started to argue, he said he was going to sue the Girl Scouts for trying to poison him…and at that point one of my wings popped out of the little match girl costume and he realized I wasn't what I seemed, probably not even a Girl Scout. He yelled something about being persecuted by the IRS and hunted by 'big government'. He pushed me out the door and down the stairs. He must have slipped himself on the top stair and the next thing I knew, he'd landed on top of me. Either he had a heart attack or knocked himself out, because he was just coming to when I rolled him off. I managed to get him into a taxi and paid the reluctant driver three full fares to take him to the hospital…and I'm not sure but what he's either dying or dead, so I thought I ought to let you know."

With mixed emotions, Satan saw the sense of defeat sweep over those majestic features, the twinkle disappear from the omniscient eye, and he actually felt a little sad. He'd won, of course. And he did look forward to having evil Orville sitting at his left hand from whence he could see to it that the air conditioning continued to malfunction…still…oh well…better luck next time. "Well," he said, "I'll be off now to collect the soul, because, unless I'm mistaken, he won't more than make it into the emergency room, and souls are best when they're fresh and not pumped full of drugs. It is sort of appropriate that evil Orville who never did a single uncalculated good deed, should in the end be my best Christmas present."

They shook hands, agreed to meet again in another millennium, and parted…the Almighty for the cumulus and nimbus of paradise, Satan for the hospital and his Christmas gift. Hopefully his assistants would already be at work, unscrewing the corners of the soul and gently detaching it from the body, wiping it clean of the mind.

"Well, Job," he thought to himself as he approached the hospital entry, "evil Orville's proved to be of sterner stuff." He even paused to rub his hands together and create a counterfeit ten dollar bill, which he dropped into the pot of the bell-ringing Santa standing there.

"Thank you and may the Almighty bless you," said Santa.

"He already has," laughed Satan, "but he wasn't very happy about it." As he reached for the glass door, a nurse pushed it hard open and almost knocked him down.

"Excuse me," she said to the red-faced stranger as she shoved a wad of bills into the bell-ringer's pot, "just fulfilling a last request." She quickly dashed back inside.

In the emergency room, the now invisible Satan found his assistants gathered around the table upon which Orville was in the process of exiting. They were heatedly arguing with one of the greater angels from the upper echelons.

"What's going on?" he demanded. "This soul is mine! Leave at once or I'll report you to you know who!"

"Not is yours, was yours…and he's the one sent me here in a flash as soon as he, in his omniscience, realized what was about to happen!"

"And just what is about to happen?" demanded Satan.

"Well, nothing more nor less than that Orville, as the taxi driver and one of the orderlies helped him stagger in past the bellboy out there, must have realized his life insurance was running out, because when they started to put him on a stretcher he pulled a wad of bills out of his wallet and asked the nurse to quickly give it to the bell-ringer. It looks like Orville's left you in the lurch, but the boss says no hard feelings…and he's looking forward to a rematch in a millennium or so."

"Evil Orville, evil Orville," sighed Satan, "how fickle are the ways of men." Unfolding his great black wings he ascended into the night sky above the city lights twinkling like a million stars back at the darkness.

In Therapy

Prologue

Acarya Sankara (788-820 CE), the great philosopher of Advaita Vedanta in India, understood the nature of the world to be non-dualistic, for all is Brahma. Of course, as he noted, this does not 'appear' to be the case when one uses one's senses to observe the multiplicity and diversity of the things around one. No, this was an insight that could be attained only when one sees this multiplicity as the Maya or illusion of Cosmic Consciousness. He felt that in order to attain this heightened awareness, one must first superimpose diversity upon experiences, just as Brahma does, then shift one's awareness from such 'superimpositions to the singular possibility of superimposing', for it is this which makes all the superimpositions of Maya possible. As he notes in his Commentary upon the Vedanta Sutras of Badarayana:

> "It is a matter not requiring any proof that the object and the subject whose respective spheres are the notion of the 'Thou' (the Non-Ego) and the 'Ego', and which are opposed to each other as much as darkness and light are, cannot be identified. All the less can their respective attributes be identified. Hence it follows that it is wrong to superimpose upon the subject – whose Self is intelligence, and which has for its sphere the notion of the Ego – the object whose sphere is the notion of the Non-Ego, and the attributes of the object, and vice versa to super-impose the subject and the attributes of the subject on the object. In spite of this it is on the part of man a natural procedure – which has its cause in wrong knowledge – not to distinguish the two entities (object and subject) and their respective

attributes, although they are absolutely distinct, but to superimpose upon each the characteristic nature and the attributes of the other, and thus, coupling the Real and the Unreal, to make use of expressions such as 'That am I', 'That is mine'."[1]

Jack's a perfect husband. He's good to the children. He's, you know…about that other thing…what married people do. He is a real man. That's not it. It's more me, I think. We've always talked about everything. I have no secrets, except for this. You understand, it doesn't have anything to do with Jack, and I wasn't sure I should tell him.

It's this place where I work. I'm a secretary for BMS. They have a lot of secretaries, but I'm a specialist. The "Copy Secretary". I do all the copying and proofreading on contracts and submissions. That is, I run the copier, you know. I was especially trained on the machine and anymore I'm the only one they'll let near it.

Jack calls me his 'copy cat', isn't that cute? Of course it bothers him because lots of times there's more to do than I can get done in an eight-hour day. Sometimes we have a big rush on contracts or things and I work overtime in the evening.

Jack doesn't like that so much because it leaves him with the children. Jack Junior is six. That's the boy. And Mary just turned four. That's our baby girl. They never give him any trouble, he says. But it means he can't go out, you know, and do the things men do. Like the clubs and things. He's a member of the Elks.

But we need the money for the car and house payments. I absolutely have to work and we've talked it all over together before. Besides, the Company wouldn't have spent all that time training me if they'd thought I was going to be a quitter. I've told Jack that.

It's just that sometimes the kids get on his nerves in the evenings. I will be the first to admit that when I've worked till ten or eleven at night in that office all by myself copying documents and contracts I'm just not too fresh either. He puts the kids to bed so I don't have to do that when I get home. Jack is such a dear.

And that's the problem…I mean the office and me copying there all alone four evenings in the week. It's…well, I don't know how to put it really. You see we have this copying machine. It's a new BMS 330. That's one of the top models out, and although it's quite complicated, it's our best selling model. We're selling an awful lot of them now. We send out as many as ten in a single shipment. It weighs a ton.

Well…you know how people get attached to things like cars and things? And they have real personalities. Honestly, they do! Now most people would laugh at the idea. But it's true. For example, when it's cold, my Ford won't start if I don't talk to it and coax it right along. Jack kids me about that. He's not very mechanically minded.

He can't even fix the electric can opener. When something happens, he leaves it for me. He feeds the kids peanut butter and jelly sandwiches. And that's not good for them. I've told him that before.

That's the way it is at the office, my copier I mean. The BMS 330. Why, Al's like a real person. We talk and talk all day when we're working together. Of course not out loud. The others would laugh. But we know what the other is thinking and…it sounds kind of funny to say this about a machine, but it's true. Of course our relationship is very professional. Or at least I've always thought of it that way. After all Al is a machine. That doesn't mean he can't feel like we can. Why not if cars can do it? I mean, he's not really just a machine! And about two months ago…our relationship…we got very fond of each other.

I mean honestly. Not like Jack and me. Jack is a wonderful dear with the children and all. But Alfred has…the way I tingle all over when I'm pushing a contract into his copier. And the way he lights up and gets excited when I push his buttons. I'm awfully gentle, you know. Jack has always said that. "You're just the gentlest kitten in the whole world," he says.

But Alfred is different. He really appreciates it. My fingers get warm and my heart starts beating real fast when he goes to work, just because I touched him in a certain way. I know he wouldn't behave the same way for someone else. A month ago when I was sick and one of the other girls was going to do some copying...Al didn't know her from Adam. He told me later he figured she was just after my job. Well, he certainly showed her! Absolutely refused to give her a clean copy of anything. Finally destroyed a contract right under her nose. Tore it up! That's the God's truth!

That brazen creature left the next day when I got back. Alfred was still mad. It took me all morning to get him back into a good mood.

But it's gotten serious. I mean between us. He...I...he wanted me...I don't know how to say it...it's so personal and all...I'm so mixed up...he wanted me...yes he did! He really wanted me. You know what I mean. Two weeks ago he begged me to...to undress...right there in front of him! With the copy-plate uncovered!

Naturally, I couldn't do that! I wouldn't! There wasn't anybody else in the office. It was late at night. But what would Jack think if he ever found out. That's what I told Alfred.

But it didn't stop at that. A week ago after I thought we were both being more professional...I had worked all day on a special shipment. The papers were all wrong and had to be done over. I agreed to stay and redo them. I called Jack and told him I would be very late.

It was all right at first. Then he started acting sort of funny, Alfred I mean. I could feel the room getting warmer. I didn't want to let on I noticed. You see, to excite him. Pretty soon he...he ordered me, *ordered me* to undress! And...I don't know what was the matter with me, but I did it. The heat was so unbearable. Then he...oh, I'm so ashamed...he made me crawl up on the copying tray...and then he...oh, he did terrible things...things that Jack would never do...he pulled and pinched my...and my breasts into the copier...and...copied them! The green light blinded me and I couldn't see, but I could feel him grinding and grabbing me in the tray...and then...then...oh, it's too terrible!

In Therapy

I…and night after night…I lied that I had lots of work to do. I lied to Jack and our wonderful children. I worked for nothing. He is cruel…Alfred I mean. Relentless. But I can't live without him! I can't stop. I'm losing weight. I make terrible mistakes in my work. I'm afraid somebody will find out about us. I nap during the day at my desk. I claim headaches and go home sometimes in the morning to sleep.

But that's not the worst of it…it's unbelievable…two days ago Alfred…I found out the awful truth! About Alfred, I mean. He just out and told me the morning I went in with the Ford contracts that we were through! Like that! Through! That he'd…he was…he'd been searching for an identity, that's all. That's what he said, "…searching for an identity and now I've found it." That's all he wanted me for!

And I thought it was something else! Something good and beautiful! And now suddenly he says, "I'm a woman now and we can't go on seeing each other this way, it's immoral!" He says it's *immoral*! And now he's a *woman*! He's not! He stole my identity, that's all. Those are my breasts he's got in there on his plate somewhere! They're not his…he's not a woman! But I can't reason with him. He won't let me in the room. Yesterday he clicked at me. Clicked at *me*!

My whole life is ruined. I…what will I do now? I'll lose my job! What can I tell Jack? I can't get into bed with him anymore. He sleeps on the couch anyway. What can I tell him? He's so understanding. What can I tell him about us? That Alfred's a woman? I can't go on!

But I can't live without Alfred…I can't live without copying and he won't let me…he clicks at me…he claims he's a woman! I'll…I'll…I'll drop a hairpin into his crack where it says "use no paper clips"…I'll…I'll unplug that motherfuckingbastard's 'identity search'! I'll show him who's a woman and who's a machine!

The Bedbug
or
Cimex Lactularius meets Gregor Samsa

Prologue

As upright walking and stalking mammals, human beings, without giving such actions a second thought, tend to ignore or swat or step upon the least of our fellow inhabitants of the world. As the ant laments in the Persian *Gulistan of Sa'di*...

> "I am that ant which is trodden under foot
> Not that wasp, the pain of whose sting causes lament.
> How shall I give due thanks for the blessing
> That I do not possess the strength of injuring mankind?"[1]

The Indian *Panchatantra* reminds us that there are stark and terrible punishments that await those who so thoughtlessly assault these innocent creatures:

> "The holy first commandment runs –
> Not harsh, but kindly be –
> And therefore lavish mercy on
> Mosquito, louse, and flea.
> Why speak of hurting innocence?
> For he, with purpose fell
> Who injures even noxious beasts,
> Is plunged in ghastly hell."[2]

The Hebrew scriptures demonstrate the power and majesty of these smallest of creatures when they are put to God's uses in punishing the wicked and the wanton:

> "...the Lord himself will give you a sign: behold, a virgin shall conceive, and bear a son, and shall call his name Immanuel. Butter and honey shall he eat, when he knoweth to refuse the evil, and choose the good.

"... And it shall come to pass in that day, that Jehovah will hiss for the fly that is in the uttermost part of the rivers of Egypt, and for the bee that is in the land of Assyria. And they shall come, and shall rest all of them in the desolate valleys, and in the clefts of the rocks, and upon all thorn hedges, and upon all pastures."

(*Isaiah* 7:12-190)

Now hold on there a minute! You're upset and I certainly would be too if our places were reversed...especially after shelling out as much as you paid for first class accommodations in a first class hotel, and in the executive suite on the top floor at that. Certainly you wouldn't expect to find the likes of me, a bedbug, lurking in the bed sheets, a talking bedbug, even, but this isn't going to help or even undo what's been done, and if you'll let me, I can explain.

"Fast," you say, "make it fast buddy!" Well...I'll certainly try if you're willing to listen because the other way, you know...what you're thinking of doing...that really won't help if you don't know what you're in for.

Now, then, if you're willing to listen, it would make things easier for me if you'd watch your thumbnail. Sort of move it over a bit. Don't worry, I promise not to run. I couldn't anyway seeing as how you've broken both of my back legs. Of course, I can grow new ones, but it takes time and is always a hormonal bother.

Where to begin? I suppose at the beginning might be best. I'll start with wisest Aristotle who realized that all creatures have souls...the plants, the least of the bugs, the animals, and yes, you humans too. Of course he missed the boat when it came to identifying how many souls each of these creatures had. The Jains were nearer the mark when they gave us three senses and a self. Aristotle was wrong about another thing too – no soul survives the body unless some great deed of selfless good carries it beyond that line where the fire goes when it goes out. This possibility, which Aristotle missed, is open to any soul at any level at any time who performs such an act. There's no 'ends justify the means' in the scheme of things, it's always 'the means justify the ends'.

In that place beyond where the fire goes when it goes out, there are many of the least…the miniscule and despised gnat whose buzzing through the last long night beneath the Bodhi tree kept Gautama wakeful in his meditation, and so helped hold the dreaded, many sleep-headed Mara of evil at bay…the gnat whose tiny shredded wings fell in the first light of morning like snow upon the calm brow of the enlightened Buddha. There you'll find the courageous leader of the locusts who turned his band into the land of Egypt and who was the first to fall beneath the rose-scented sandal of the oppressive pharaoh as he stamped in rage on the marbled floor of his bath. There is the patient and enduring bee who placed its life and little stinger into the rambunctious ass that Saul, the flunky of priests and the stoner of Stephen, rode on the way to Damascus where he was "breathing threatening and slaughter against the disciples of the Lord." Thrown to the ground, Saul became Paul, the Jew became a Greek…though Paul never made it to that place where the bee and the ass lie down in eternal peace.

And there you will find the bluebottle fly that flung its insignificant being into the poisoned ointment sent by a jealous and desperate suitor of the saintly Clothilda, virgin of Magdeberg – "a salve," the scoundrel said, to rub upon her chapped and torn hands in the fields where she labored pulling turnips in the frosty winter for the poor and starving. And with the blessed fly is that small and dedicated army of crabs whose struggling kept at bay the terrible and tempting visions of St. Anthony as these sought to lure him into sin. There you will find those brave lions whose empty, hungry bellies cried to the heavens, yet still they refused to eat Daniel when Darius the Persian ordered him thrown into their den…and who were flayed by the cruel court satraps and turned into riding boots… there the humble ants who taught Indra the absurdity of building palaces in paradise…and there those shy squid whose crushed and drained bodies provided Mohammed the ink with which to take the dictates of the Archangel…

It is a great gathering of the least…and I, a bedbug…what am I doing there? And why am I here? Alas, because I have no selfless act to my credit, only one single act of opportunistic shame. It is my curse and my reward. I too have a soul, an immortal soul, which I would gladly shed…

You see, I…my family, a discreet and gentle folk, for generations shared a house with one of the oldest families in Judea…decent, reserved. We were taught to cooperate with our hosts, to disturb their sleep as little as possible and only at certain ritual times…to respect the women and children of the house and never to bother the adults in their multiplying. We all lived in harmony until one day a dreadful plague swept through the village and our hosts were forced to flee. And as they fled, they sold what could not be taken with them. The aging blanket in which I and my immediate family lived was traded to a dealer in lame and crippled animals destined for the slaughter. Thus began a life of chaos and change in which we were forced to live in closest proximity with sheep ticks whose coarse gorging is an abomination. We were tormented and teased by lice who hung their egg cases willy-nilly like dirty laundry on any passing hair follicle, snapped at by rats who held us accountable for the torments inflicted by their fleas.

Alas, all of my family perished, and I alone lived on in an abandoned stable in a tattered hanging rag that had become my winding sheet. There I awaited my end in starving loneliness.

Then, one winter night, the sagging, dusty room was suddenly filled with voices and people stumbling into one another in the darkness. Finally, a little pile of straw was set aflame and by its smoky light my rag was seized and tossed with others into a broken manger to make a resting pad for a newborn infant. We had always been taught to respect women and children…but my hunger had blinded me…and I took but a single sip, a single small drop from the littlest of the little toes where I was sure it would not be missed.

Ah, that was my undoing…for it was no mortal flesh and it had no taste like any other I had known! My body seemed to be both ice and fire at once! That single drop rose again and again in my throat as I sought to expel it…but I couldn't. Then it radiated sparks into all of my six legs and they began to twitch uncontrollably. Suddenly the room exploded in a flashing ball of fire and I found myself surrounded by great gaunt birds that I was certain would devour me. I later realized they were angels of the first through sixteenth hierarchies gathered to judge me for the sacrilege I had committed.

I was not to be destroyed. No, my punishment was far more terrible. A philosopher, with whom I later once spent the night, said that we are what we eat…and it was this had both saved and condemned me. A microscopic portion of my being had become divine. The rest of me retained its physical and carnal nature. I could not be killed, but I could not be fully admitted to that paradise of the good and selfless! To be a schizophrenic in paradise is a cruel thing – one is unaccepted, yet tolerated, a necessary evil in the midst of necessary good. No one has ever touched me or even threatened me to my face…but when my back is turned, the greater angels make smacking noises and the little ones blow winds at my back as though from descending fly-swatters. I do not belong and yet cannot escape.

I pleaded with them to end my misery…to admit me or to cast me down into those terrible hells where creatures go whose only act on earth is a great and evil one…or to extinguish me entirely with the faceless souls of creatures who achieve neither good nor evil. Finally, my request was heard, and I was told that it had been decided at the highest level that for one night every year, that birth night of my act, I was to be returned to earth to be again the creature I had been then, the one part of my nature that I still was. This has been my fate for hundreds of years and so here I am again this eve.

I did not want to disturb you, for I have despaired of all hope. I never mean to disturb those I find myself with at this time…whether they be kings or popes or hot dog vendors…but my desire overcomes me and my physical self takes over. When I am caught, I am a coward and am afraid and seek to escape…or, barring that, to whine and plead my tragic case in the hope that perhaps with extreme compassion my host for the evening can somehow free me. But tonight I am so tired…the centuries have robbed me of my cowardice and my pleading. Do as you will…my shell is yours…release that single tiny drop if you can.

The Second Coming

Prologue

The lot of all sentient beings, the Buddha said, is suffering. Its sources are both in us, created by our desires, and outside of us, sent by the world in which we find ourselves. According to the book of *Job*, such suffering may be a test designed by Satan in a wager made with God. The text upon which Job and other songs of lamentation are based is generally assumed to be that of the ancient Babylonian *Poem of the Righteous Sufferer*, in which the poet's woes are greater than even his Gods' abilities to help:

"...a tempest is driving me!
Debilitating Disease is let loose upon me:
An Evil Wind has blown [from the] horizon,
Headache has sprung up from the surface of the underworld,"

———————

"They have wrenched my neck muscles and taken the
strength from my neck.
They struck [my chest,] drubbing my breast.
They affected my flesh and caused convulsions,
[In] my epigastrium they kindled a fire."

———————

"My lofty stature they destroyed like a wall,
My robust figure they laid down like a bulrush,
I am thrown down like a bog plant and cast on my face."[1]

It was impossible to determine whether the parallel lines that crossed early Wednesday morning two and a half feet from the southwest curb at First and Broadway were drawn on some other planet by some other life form or originated on earth and were ricocheted back to First and Broadway from an imperceptible spatial warp at the edge of the universe. The consequences of their one-dimensional intersection were so catastrophic for Dr. George Watson, who was two and a half feet from the southwestern curb, that he rarely considered the possible positions of their source.

The immediate meeting of the lines at that point occupied by the good philosophy professor was not in itself dramatic. He felt what he thought was a slight earth tremor. Only at his office, when he glanced into the mirror behind the secretary's desk, did he notice anything extraordinary. He first suspected a fracture in the glass...one half of the reflection appeared to have slipped ahead of the other...as in a bad casting job where the difference in the halves, expressed in a coarse seam, mars the final product.

His finger, first on the glass and then on his forehead, convinced him that indeed the two halves of his body no longer fit nicely and tightly together.

It was early in the day. Mrs. Corson had not yet arrived at the office. He locked the door and hastily stripped to examine the rest of his body. The seam went all the way from the roots of his hair through his crotch and up his backside. The left half slightly advanced over the right. Even his penis was so fractured. This proved one of the most disconcerting aspects of his affliction, for when he urinated the seam tended to deflect the stream in a sharp right angle over the front of his pants.

There was no blood, though he thought there should have been, as after an operation, and there had been no pain. He inspected himself carefully and concluded he was not seeing things. He denied the possibility of a miracle of any sort. As a philosopher he dimly suspected what had happened. It was not necessary to consult either a psychiatrist or a physician.

He began wearing high collars and a Scottish hunting cap so the shift was visible to his students only as it crossed his face, parting the mustache hairs to fall away from the nose and into the mouth, where it forked the tongue slightly.

His students were too polite to comment upon the sudden furrow between his eyes, but by the end of a month they had abandoned the first two rows of seats. Some of the girls were paler in his presence and behaved as though he upset their stomachs.

At the beginning of the second semester he saw that he definitely sickened some and fascinated others. The composition of his classes changed. Instead of the bright minds he once had drawn, now he drew a weird collection of masochists, addicts and individuals traversing late and problematical puberty. These came to feed upon his scar tissue, not upon his wisdom.

His colleagues abandoned the faculty club at his appearance and stammered in his presence if he did happen to trap one of them. Toward the middle of May his wife sought a separation on the grounds of mental cruelty. She left, taking the children.

The split neither increased nor decreased. Nor did it, apart from mental anguish, afford him pain. His internal organs, though he suspected they were also fractured, continued to function normally and gave him no cause for worry.

However, at the end of two semesters he had had enough. He realized things couldn't continue thus – something had to be done. Why should he bear the world's sick snickers and sicker horror at his condition?

But what could he do?

He was certain what had happened now, and suddenly the rectification of his tragedy was quite clear. Parallel lines are one-dimensional, but two-directional. And, extending infinitely in reverse of either direction, they must cross again in a curved universe...cross in endless cycles in fact, unless somehow terminated at their crossing, as in his case.

Simply, then, he needed to be at the corner of First and Broadway, two and a half feet from the southwestern curb, when their planes merged again, moving in reverse of their direction the first time.

As soon as the semester was over he took up his watch at the corner. He wasn't scheduled to teach summer courses, so he had time for his quest.

He wore the same clothes he had worn then, attempted to think the same thought. And to leave, unless memory failed him, the same foot on the curbing. He would walk forward the two and a half feet...stop...walk backward to the sidewalk...forward again. Every third day he took his shirt to a local laundry to be washed and pressed.

He had fixed the time of his first accident at between six and seven-thirty a.m. For margin he added one hour to either end plus one for daylight saving time. He walked four and one half hours every day.

Of course he became something of a curiosity and a traffic hazard. People drove out of their way to watch him. The street grew more and more congested, the air polluted by exhaust. The pavement buckled here and there at the increased use. It also became more dangerous for the professor. Where earlier people had swerved to avoid him, rowdies now swerved to scare him, and on one occasion actually knocked him down. However, his need was greater than his fear of the swooping cars. At the end of a month the city tired of the spectacle and returned to other more direct routes.

He waited through the summer and into the autumn, taking just enough time away from his station after the middle of September to occasionally modify one of his lectures on 'Wittgenstein and the New Left'.

Nothing happened...and continued to not happen.

As his senses grew more keen with his anticipation, he believed on early winter mornings, when the traffic was still, he could hear the lines slicing through space with a high canted whistle. Other times he thought he noticed the heavens splitting in the distance at their passing. Once an earth tremor fooled him so he ran home to his mirror.

The winter was turning severe. He began to wear earmuffs and an overcoat. 'Wittgenstein and the New Left' was almost done.

About ten days before the end of the semester in December, the city was bludgeoned by the heaviest snowfall in the memory of its inhabitants. Traffic snarled. Cars were abandoned. Streets were closed. Because of the wind currents racing from two directions, the drifts at the corner of First and Broadway were almost insurmountable.

He had continued his march through the early morning, until the large flakes began to fall so heavily he couldn't see and was afraid of missing his direction. Confronted with the choice of remaining at his point two and a half feet from the curb, or missing the lines for perhaps another cycle, he chose to wait. He wrapped his coat more tightly about his shoulders and stamped his feet until the snow became too heavy and it was easier just to stand.

After a while the waiting became warmer. The cramps in his legs eased somewhat. Over the groaning of the storm he could hear the lines approaching. Soon, perhaps he would be normal again.

The whiteout was complete as the low wind coming down First flung its swirling flakes at the high wind racing up Broadway. At the intersection they competed for possession of the crossing, ranted at him to arbitrate their dispute.

Above the winds the whine of the lines grew stronger as they accelerated backward at nearly the speed of light. He could see the flash even through the snow.

Later, when the storm abated and the plows made it to the intersection of First and Broadway, they found the core of the drifts had melted during the night and refrozen into a small pond. Two rosy earmuff halves eyed one another across the ice.

The Ecumenical Cruise 2020 A.D.
or
(The Revolt of the Angels?)

Prologue

This story begins with the 'earth', for in many of the world's religions it is from the earth that human beings arise, just as it is to the earth that they return. And it is the gods who are responsible for this mysterious transformation of clay. In China, for example, the goddess Nu Wa made a muddy slurry from the fertile yellow soil of the great central plain and from this yellow slurry fashioned women and men who under her guidance began begetting at once. In another less happy Chinese version, the God P'an-ku also fashioned men and women of clay, but before he was done a rainstorm damaged many of them. This is the source of the deformed and lame. The Yoruba creator God, Obatala, was busily molding individuals in the hot sun when he became very thirsty and drank too much palm wine. This led to the distorted nature of the last people that he made.

In an ancient Hebrew tale, when Gabriel was sent by God to secure dust from the earth to create man, the earth absolutely refused him. When the angel asked why, she, anticipating her future, replied that she would be cursed and tormented by man, so if God wanted her dust for this creature, He himself would have to take it. She would give it to no other. The result was that God reached down and with His own hand "took the dust of the ground, and created the first man therewith."[1]

The story proceeds from the creation of human beings to the origins of the gods themselves and to the question: "Did the gods fashion human beings from clay and dust, or did human beings so fashion their gods?" One answer is provided by the pre-Socratic Greek philosopher, Xenophanes of Colophon, who observed that if oxen or lions possessed hands so that they could paint and sculpt like human beings, they would paint and sculpt their gods with bodies like their own: the gods of horses would be portrayed as horses, the gods of oxen as oxen. Among human beings, Africans have gods that are dark with black hair and snub noses, while the blond Thracians portray their gods with light skin, blue eyes and reddish hair. However, beyond the relativity of these perspectives, he believed that God was a unity quite unlike either the gods or human beings. As one, it is the totality that thinks and sees and hears and sets all in motion with mind.[2]

Relating the realm of the divine to that of the human are the keepers of the faiths, the practitioners of belief systems, the religious leaders of the nations and tribes. Some of these are gods themselves as in the case of the Hindu Brahmin priests who, according to the *Laws of Manu*,[3] are, by origin and nature, gods among the gods, and their authoritative teaching carries the full weight of the Vedas. Others are men who have been deified. This was the case with the Sumerian hero, Utnapishtim, who with his sacrifices saved the gods themselves at the end of the great flood unleashed upon the world by Enlil. When the gods gathered "like flies" at the smells rising from his sacrifice, Enlil, who was at first angered, finally responded to the pleading of the deities and raised Utnapishtim and his wife to divine status.[4] Still others are human beings who have been given the divine capacity and power to control things both in heaven and on earth. As Jesus said to his Apostles: "Verily I say unto you, what things soever ye shall bind on earth shall be bound in heaven; and what things soever ye shall loose on earth shall be loosed in heaven."[5]

Finally our story leads us to the great Ecumenical Cruise of the new millennium and the events that followed from it. For this portion of its telling it relies upon the reminiscences of two old friends, Munkar and Nakir, the examining angels that, according to the Muslim theologian, Imam-I-A'zam Abu Hanifa, visit Muslims in their graves to pose questions as to the nature and depth of their souls' faith. The Imam tells us:

"The graves of those who will give precise answers will enlarge and a window will be opened to Paradise.

Every morning and every evening they will see their places in Paradise, and angels will do them favors and give them good news. He who cannot answer precisely…His grave will become so tight that he will feel as if his bones would intertwine."[6]

But Munkar and Nakir are not the only angels to visit the earth – religious texts and traditions around the world speak of such visits. For example, a Jewish legend tells us that in the distant past angels from heaven looked down and saw the daughters of man and were overcome by desire and lust. Under the leadership of twenty angel captains, they accordingly descended to the earth where they then mated with these daughters. The end result was a race of giants who threatened to overpower their human counterparts.[7]

For those who have never been to paradise, or even thought much about it, it is needful to know, as I have it from Munkar and Nakir, that there is, or at least was, a Bridge of the Separator which connects things of this world with things of that. In the center of this Bridge of the Separator is a Barzakh that demarcates the spectrum of visible from the spectrum of invisible light. The term 'barzakh' itself can be related to *Surah* 55:19 of the *Koran*, where it is likened to the line that divides salt and fresh water, but which in its nature is neither salt nor fresh. The word 'barzakh' also describes that invisible boundary between the world of human beings, the earth, and the heavens, the spirit world and God.[8]

And now to the Ecumenical Cruise itself…

The Cruise

It would be difficult to identify the specific origins of the great Ecumenical Cruise launched to celebrate the advent of the new millennium. Its roots are surely to be found in every religious conflict from pre-history up to the end of the twentieth century, roots put down wherever on battlefields or in the ruins of smoking villages violence was used to appease or avenge or demonstrate the will and/or power of a god or gods. These roots took hold in soil fertilized by the blood of exhausted combatants and on altars made slippery by human or animal sacrifice. Whenever and wherever there emerged even a grudging awareness of the 'other' and a minimal acceptance of the other's rites and rituals, there and then ecumenism began to sprout. Of course, its growth was halted again and again by crusades East or West, religious wars, Aryan massacres of Dravidians, Confucian persecutions of Buddhists, temple burnings, savage inter-tribal raids among the world's indigenous peoples – aided and abetted by groups' or societies' beliefs in their deities. There would come pauses in the violence, recesses with covenants, treaties, agreements, arrangements, compromises, conventions, and new revelations on old revelations. However, almost immediately forces would regroup and renew the struggles in a kind of thesis – anti-thesis – synthesis dance of death around the altars of the gods. Still, all in all, after each paroxysm things seemed a little better – for example, black human beings could enter the paradises of white human beings, women no longer needed to become men in order ascend into heaven.

In the twentieth century, however, the last century of the past millennium, economic forces and social realities had accelerated great changes. Catholics talked to Protestants in most countries, even though each realized the error of the other. Hindus tolerated Buddhists. Brahmins spoke to Dalits – at least at election time. Gradually a worldwide movement emerged, supported by industrialists, bankers, and politicians, to end religious conflicts and seek the basic commonalties, if any, in the religions of all societies in the name of prosperity in the new global economy. It was agreed at last to convene a World Congress of Beliefs that would encompass all groups and perspectives, no matter how great or small, national or tribal, to bring religious leaders together. But where? No place could be agreed upon, and so the idea of an 'ecumenical cruise' was born – a vessel flying no national flags, visiting no ports between departure and return, steaming around the world! It would be a voyage of arguments and arrangements among all groups, and, hopefully, it would ultimately produce a modus vivendi and a constitution for a parliament of united world religions.

Demonstrating the more devout side of capitalism, the Cunard Lines made the Queen Elizabeth II available for this momentous attempt to bring together the leaders of all faiths everywhere. For the duration of her spiritual voyage she had been renamed the Quest for Enlightenment II – the first quest referred symbolically to the origins and revelations of the various belief systems of her passengers. In New York, with funds provided by the Rockefeller Foundation and the Ford Foundation, the QEII galleries and luxury staterooms were divided into sections and redecorated in simple but pious blue-gray. Great suites were partitioned into small sleeping and meditation cells. Restaurants and gift shops gave way to libraries and worship centers where ritual and rite videos could also be projected. This was a particularly important condition for those faiths that relied upon live animal sacrifice or human circumcision and other mutilation rituals in their religious ceremonies. Thus, if only vicariously, the celebrant could, by viewing a video, still relate to the divine power and/or forces upon which his or her particular belief system relied.

Scientists and engineers were brought in from East and West and North and South to design the accommodations and equipment for the voyage. Ethnologists, anthropologists, and consultants from various religious and cultural groups came to work on matters pertaining to diet and other ritual affairs.

The worldwide interest in the ecumenical cruise had six very genuine bases: (1) The first was a genuine feeling that some religions did have elements in common, and that these might be used to effectively proselytize in the interest of eliminating centuries of religious strife; (2) A genuine feeling that if one's group's leaders were not present the group might be excluded from whatever arrangements and covenants and spheres of influence were worked out; (3) A genuine feeling that one's group's religious perspectives were invariably better, and that if one sent one's leaders to demonstrate this view in its correct light, all others, at least those who were capable of rational thought, would see that this was so; (4) A genuine feeling that most of the others were wrong in their absurd or naive or pernicious views, and that one's group had an

Warning

obligation to send one's leaders to point this out; (5) A genuine feeling that no matter what happened or was discussed, one's group would be considered irrelevant if one's leaders didn't attend – besides, attendance would be popular at home; (6) A genuine feeling that if one's group were not represented, it might be branded a 'cult' by all the other participants.

In order to appeal to the largest possible representation, the date of departure for the Ecumenical Cruise was set at the time of the winter solstice, for this is a special time in so many different faiths.

While financial and technical support flooded in to launch this great enterprise, religious leaders from various isms and temples and ashrams, institutions, and churches around the world came together, even groups that were less clear on the nature of the gods or their existence, but which still subscribed to the idea of paradise or a 'pure land' of milk and flowers, and others who would go no further than 'a force' or 'the wind'. There were pantheists, polytheists, monotheists, monists, henotheists, dualists, idolaters, fetishists, and the president of a group that believed only that they believed that they believed. It was to be a 'theological Noah's Ark' – a ship of priests, mystics, patriarchs, rabbis, imams, ayatollahs, medicine men and women, new age seers, popes, gurus, bhikkhus, sadhus, shamans, brahmins, televangelists, channelers, mediums, et cetera.

Boarding did present some problems when the leaders of different groups arrived at the boarding area at the same time. This was resolved by a cargo crane that could lift a platform containing as many as one Roman pope, three Greek and/or Coptic patriarchs, four ayatollahs, seven assorted directors of ashrams, one rather hefty archbishop of Canterbury and one Canadian and three Ashanti medicine persons, all complete with baggage. Unfortunately there was some difficulty when the platform tilted and the Roman pope found himself in the embrace of the Sh'ia Ayatollah from Tehran. The crane operator quickly adjusted the platform as he set it down so that the favor was returned when the Ayatollah slid into His Holiness. But despite such incidents, the boarding was finally completed. It also helped that, since the sailing was to start from New York under the auspices and with the blessings of the United Nations, the New York branch of the Mafia and various other related groups agreed to establish a 'mugging free' zone for participants waiting to embark. So strictly was this enforced that not even the police, in or out of uniform, were permitted to enter and shoot or otherwise interrogate representatives from different racial groups.

The crew consisted almost entirely of females, for it was a general consensus among most theologians and gurus East/West/North/South that women have little insight into or understanding of religion because their 'conceptual' powers are chiefly limited to physical processes, whereas gifted men are able to conceive the profound insights upon which religion is based. Thus a female crew, kept apart from the few female delegates representing specific beliefs, would not interfere with the serious discussions in any way. Most of these crew members were recruited from Olympic sports contingents, for it was felt that Olympic Games testing would provide a reliable pool of drug-free, chromosomally sound young women in top physical form. The crew would also represent all nations racially and ethnically – after all, this was to be an ecumenical cruise.

Second only to the overwhelming international response to the idea of an ecumenical cruise in the new millennium was the miraculous working hand in hand of industry, science, technology, and religion in order to bring it all about. Among the vessel's most valuable innovations after it was refurbished was its highly sophisticated fueling system, which, by extracting hydrogen efficiently from sea water, permitted the ship to meet all its energy needs indefinitely without docking.

Even more important, in light of its varied passenger list, was its food handling system, which was based on a recycling process that used an initial supply of artificially created, tiny neutral pellets that were neither meat nor vegetable based. These pellets, because of their small size, basic elasticity, and ability to gel, could in the vessel's kitchens be converted into wheat flour, rice flour, locust flour, and corn meal, from which won tons, puddings, casseroles, cobblers, burritos, chapati, miso, cinnamon rolls, etc., could be produced for consumption by diners at individual tables. Each table was assigned to a particular group, and at each table devout diners had at their disposal an array of sauces, which imparted to any dish not only a desired flavor but a calorie and vitamin boost. There was ersatz meat sauce for non-vegetarians, a variety of fish and/or vegetable flavors for different vegetarians, and a selection of fruit-flavored sauces for fruitarians. Thus delicious dishes could be prepared from a common base and served to the different tastes at different tables. The tables were curtained off from one another so that Hindus would not smell beef sauces, and Muslims and Jews not smell pork sauces, etc. This situation helped to mute the highly varied ritual prayers and chants of different leaders at mealtime. The curtains also enclosed the various eating practices and noises of the different faiths.

At the end of each day this wonderful system captured and recycled the pellets once they had left the digestive tracts of the diners. They were filtered, purified, and returned to service – absolutely minus any and all impurities or hint of 'flavor sauces'. Since there was no meat, vegetable, or fruit content in these dishes, which had been prepared from coal-tar derivatives, it was felt there could be no serious objections to the system, but just to be sure, special tours of the kitchens were provided for all representatives upon boarding the vessel. It was clearly stressed in these tours that in most of the major and minor creation stories, the gods and goddesses created plants and animals and human beings from the earth, to which all organisms returned in time. Thus, no matter what one ate, one was consuming that which might have been a distant relative in some ancient age, or which had in a previous cycle existed as a plant or animal that according to present ritual proscription could not be eaten. This ingenious system functioned in providing the fuel for delegates' bodies much as the fuel system using extracted hydrogen cared for the vessel's energy needs.

This doesn't mean that everyone was completely happy with the idea of subsisting on artificial food pellets, no matter what sauces were applied to them. Some passengers objected to being fed what they considered recycled human wastes (what one Vietnamese journalist coarsely described as "theological shit"). There were, of course, some serious objections based on religious grounds. For example, a group of Orthodox Jews objected, as they said, "to being fed non-kosher Christian by-products." But these were pacified when it was made clear that Christians would also be consuming what had been processed, in a sense, through kosher Jewish digestive tracts. Muslims, Hindus, Brahmins, Dalits, Confucians, Buddhists, Shintoists, Yorubans, etc., were eventually won over by similar arguments, for after all, all wastes were purified, just as nature herself recycled all organisms, and so these foods represented the sanctity, ultimately, of their theological mission. It was also made very clear at demonstrations given at a number of points in the kitchens, that it was impossible to distinguish pellets eaten by Hindus from pellets consumed by Buddhists, pellets processed through white men from those processed through black and yellow men. In a word, the universality of the pellets came to symbolize the universality of their sacred mission, and, in view of the commitment of all to the enterprise and its success, everyone was willing to give the system a 'try'. Most passengers were pleasantly surprised and impressed by the quality and variety of meals and sauces served on board.

If the dining arrangements posed one set of problems, the quartering of the participants posed another, and one that was only partially solved when the QEII was sectioned into cubicles of the same size and color. For example, there were those who demanded a porthole as befitting the sheer numbers of their devoted followers. Others insisted that they more than made up in quality what others boasted of as quantity. This was resolved by painting all portholes black so that no one could look out. This created problems later for the firm because the paint, which had to withstand seawater, tended to etch the glass. That some decks were clearly upper and others lower also posed problems, for some monotheists insisted that they should be on top and polytheists and various others be given the lower levels. At the same time the leaders of the Pure Land Buddhist sects felt that their closeness to Amitaba Buddha qualified them for these top slots, and they suggested that certain Zen representatives should share the lower decks with the Parsees. Vedanta monists insisted that monism took precedence over monotheism, and the various polytheists and animists argued that their very worship of all categories and elements in the universe gave them the top layer, just as their beliefs related them most clearly to the entire cosmos.

Female monists who worshipped the earth mother refused to sleep anywhere near male monists chanting "Hare Krishna."

Finally, a lottery system was devised where one's space depended upon a number drawn at random. Once again the great depth of the participants' faiths saved the situation as each believed that his or her system, god, gods, powers, force fields, sacred spirits would assign the number chosen and so whatever number one drew must have considerable religious significance.

At last the great ship with its variegated load of red hats, green hats, yellow hats, fur pieces, bald heads, skull caps, burqas, hair shirts, no shirts, dhotis, loincloths, business suits, and cloaks, as well as the flags of a thousand faiths flying, the engines humming to the accompaniment of a thousand chants and mantras and prayers, sailed off with its load of the shaven and unshaven, the circumcised and the uncircumcised, the vegetarians, the carnivores, the voodooists, and the Roman pope, the medicine men and women from Zimbabwe, the President of the Really Southern Baptist Convention, etc., etc., to begin the Ecumenical Cruise. And there were not a few in the well-wishing crowd on shore who saw a sun-illumined halo like a smoke ring hovering over her stacks and upper decks.

The Disaster

At worst, in any group of disparate individuals involved in discussing and arguing themes of even the most common interest, a kind of unstable order may persist until, like iron filings clinging to an electric magnet when the power is shut down, the participants fly off in their separate directions. At best, there comes a determining moment when differences seem to coalesce, the filings come together, and disagreements are resolved. And so it was with the Ecumenical Cruise. The first two weeks out the rancor and animosity had built to such a level that one night at dinner a number of glasses and sauce bottles were flung from table to table as diners refused to draw their curtains. The next day, as the ship rounded the Cape of Good Hope on a placid sea, the assembly in the Great Hall was anything but placid. All of the representatives who could walk had gathered to vote on a very simple statement to the effect that the representatives at best could agree only to disagree on all matters relating to religious beliefs.

Halfway through the session, however, an unforeseen blockage occurred in the food recycling and processing equipment, perhaps as a result of the combination of the infinite variety of sauces – the Shona dried locust and Christmas Beetle relish mixed with Middle Eastern leek puree, bouillabaisse sauce, blue cheese, Hindu curry with pepper chutneys, and Christian Brothers burgundy, coupled with the digestive juices of so many theologians and theological positions. In any case, one of the tank casings cracked, which permitted the escape of a mixture of methane and other gases emitted from the consumed and discharged pellets being recycled from the bitter and unpleasant dinner the night before. These gases were sucked into the air-conditioning system and pumped into the vents in the Great Hall, unbeknownst to the delegates. There they induced a kind of intoxicating euphoria. As this euphoria spread, individuals who had cursed one another the night before began to embrace one another. Others laughed and wept at the same time. Many spoke in tongues. Christian hugged Muslim, Jew embraced Confucian, and gradually a sense of harmonious unity began to make itself felt in the official proceedings as well.

And so it was that someone – later reports insist that it was a Shinto priest from Nagoya – moved that the convention go on record declaring there and for all time to come that "all religions and all deities are created equal, and that all faiths lead to Paradise," so that "never again should any faith presume to take precedence over any other, nor should anyone who believed be excluded from Paradise."

This resolution was greeted with resounding cheers, which in their vehemence caused the QEII to rock from side to side. As the gas continued to spread, it affected not only the theologians and reporters in the Great Hall, but also the crew and those representatives too seasick to attend the convocation. Like an approaching storm, the momentum of this equality of all religions and all deities spread into the ship's radio system where it was broadcast to the waiting world at large. Assembled crowds collectively gasped, stunned by this enormous ecumenical step. Within moments, however, around the world collective cheers followed the shocks of disbelief. Meanwhile the signatures of the delegates, one after another, were duly affixed to this 'pax theologica' and the precious document with these signatures was placed in the ship's safe, while copies were faxed to the religious leaders' places of origin.

Late in the evening one of the kitchen mechanics discovered the cracked line and repaired it so that by the next day when the leaders arose the effects of the gas had begun to wear off. The next morning, around hundreds of breakfast tables, delegates saw what they had said and signed. Most were dazed by its enormity…"How was it possible?" "What was I thinking?" But then word began to flow back from around the world congratulating them on their courage. Clearly the only thing now was to stand boldly by their revolutionary protocol and insist that the action had been taken in deepest religious communion. Under no circumstances would it do to say or hint that one, as a leader of a flock, large or small, had acted in a fog of methane gas.

The Consequences

Some may assume with Epicurus and his atomists that the gods long ago withdrew to a far corner of the universe where they spend their eons in idle conversation with one another, oblivious to all human affairs, moved neither by sacrifice and prayer nor threat and evil deeds on earth. But this is not true, for, though religions have fathomed the mystery of "why us" in different fashions, they all illustrate in one way or another that the gods are paying attention.

Perhaps no event more clearly illustrates this point than the convening by the gods, almost immediately after the "Proclamation of Equality Among the Gods" became known both in heaven and on earth, of a divine assembly in many ways like its earthly counterpart. For the gods, of course, the issue was a bit different. They had always tolerated one another's company and visited back and forth, amusing themselves at events taking place among their followers, and boasting a bit when one group seemed to have gained an upper hand, or sending condolences to gods and goddesses whose systems had gone out of fashion or been absorbed into other systems. And, of course, all had a good laugh from time to time at the things they were supposed to have said and done.

But this time it was different. Their human protégés and followers had decreed for all time that all the gods were equal. It seemed clear, even though facilitated by a methane gas leak, that humanity had grasped something fundamental about the nature of the gods themselves. And if all gods are equal and all faiths lead to Paradise, then really anyone who makes any kind of claim on it must be allowed in, no matter how bizarre her or his religious perspectives might be. Meat eater sects could not exclude vegetarians. Those who claimed their deity had fathered a baby were as acceptable as those who saw this as blasphemy. Those whose gods had eight arms were as eligible as those whose gods had none. Horse sacrifices, chicken sacrifices, no sacrifices, reciting "Hare, Hare Krishna" or "Amitaba Buddha" or "Allah Akbar" or "Om" or speaking in tongues – all were passages to Paradise.

"But surely," objected Jehovah and Siva together, "there must be some sort of entrance requirement...a test that is universally applicable?"

Allah thought for a moment, then said, "I have an idea...but first I must speak with Munkar and Nakir."

Reminiscences of Munkar and Nakir

"...and that was it! That's how it began! Allah knew he could count on us, you see, because Nakir and I had been His 'proctoring angels' for centuries. Now, there are those who believe the life of an angel is easy...if one can carry a tune and harmonize on a hosanna or an "Allah Akbar" while flitting from nimbus to cumulus..."

"...But Munkar here and I can assure anyone, from our experiences, there is damned little chanting and flitting and lots of hard work."

"Right. Of course, there were angels who had easy assignments...taking coded messages and revelations to one prophet or another or facilitating a pregnancy or curing a bout of impotence, helping a shepherd find a lost water buffalo, determining the winner in an interfaith basketball game, helping students pass finals...but those were exceptions."

"You see, back when Allah and Mohammed fenced off a special Muslim section of Paradise, we were put in charge of admissions. I don't know what screening mechanisms other religions used for the candidates for their sections, but we can tell you that SATs, LCATs and MEDCAT exams were nothing compared to ours!"

"In fact, one could pass all those and still flunk ours, and a large number of Muslims who successfully passed the law school and university exams and earned Ph.D.s and M.D.s, and Th.D.s failed ours. I don't know whether the Christians or Jews or Hindus or Buddhists had the same failure rates or not, but we were strict."

"No one, and I mean no one, got into heaven – at least the Muslim heaven – without coming through us. We were the line between believers and unbelievers, practitioners and backsliders, the final filter between Paradise and that other place."

"It was like this…after the funeral, friends and family would leave the body with the soul still in it in the tomb. Then we would show up to administer the 'final exam'. In order to get its full attention right off, Munkar here would roll his eyes back up into his head and wiggle his pointed ears…and I would whistle through my nose, kind of soft-like, then slowly louder…and both of us would grind and gnash our teeth…"

"In those days we wore our hair longer in dreadlocks and could will them to stand up and dance around on our heads while our ears went in circles. After a minute or two of this, old body would usually open one eye a slip and the soul would peep out to see what was going on. Most of them couldn't really believe they were dead…maybe it was a bad dream, a nightmare with Munkar and Nakir in it. But once the gnashing of teeth increased a notch and the ears were going so fast they became a blur…and the nose whistling was like a jet taking off…both eyes would pop open and soul would realize it was for real. Not a dream! Even the densest backsliders recognized where they were and who we were…"

"There was a lot of nonsense in circulation about us. Some of it put out by infidels and some of it produced by other angels who resented our position…calling us names like 'grave gropers' and 'tomb thumpers'…"

"…incidentally, that stuff about Munkar as Mr. Pleaser and me as Master Squeezer…all lies! It's true, of course, that if folks passed their entrance examinations, then the earth would roll back a bit and suddenly rugs and a divan and a pitcher of fresh water and a bouquet of roses would be brought in by Jinns who also opened a little window to let the soul see into Paradise."

"And it's also true that the earth, when a soul flunked the exams, would sort of sidle up and squash body about a bit. But 'Mr. Pleaser' and 'Master Squeezer'…that's absurd. Gabriel told us that 'squeezing' was part of an agreement that the Chief had worked out with the earth when He borrowed some of her dust in order to make human beings in the first place. The squeezing was in compensation for all the abuse and nasty things they would do to poor nature, like the Romans sowing salt in Carthage after they had burned it…or the modern practice of sowing land mines willy-nilly over field and fen…"

"In the beginning, it was quite simple really. After Mohammed designed the program with the Chief, we were sent down to the graves and tombs and told to cross-examine all applicants for entry into this new Islamic afterlife. Those who passed the test got in, those who flunked went…well you know. At first there was only one paradise for all Muslims. But when Mohammed died…of course he passed the test because he had written most of it…well, when he died, the trouble started. We began to get all sorts of curious characters claiming to be Muslim…Shi'ites and Sunnis and Kharijites and Zaidites and Assassins and Ismailies, and Sufis…like Omar said, the representatives from 'two and seventy jarring sects'."

"We asked the Chief what we should do. His solution was both simple and wonderful: 'Why, we'll subdivide Paradise, segregate the groups…a Sunni heaven, a Shi'ite Paradise, a Sufi afterlife, a Kharijite other world'. So when the mourners left a body, once we got its attention, we would note its affiliation on the top of the forms, and take it from there."

"In bad years with many Muslims killing Muslims, Shi'ites warring on Sunnis and vice versa in struggles over the Caliphate, there would be lots of candidates requiring different versions of the exam for their section of Paradise. But we kept up. We became so good we could tell a Sunni from a Shi'ite from a Sufi from a hookah just by the way the toes curled when the body came in. The Shi'ite toes wrapped themselves into conservative little balls, Sunni toes tended to spread out...with Kharijites the toes on the right foot would be trying to strangle the toes on the left, and with the Zaidites it was the other way around. With the Sufis and the Dervishes, the toes were still dancing when we approached the body."

"...Gabriel told us one day that the Chief actually got the multiple heavens solution from the deities of other religions like the Christians who had Catholic and Protestant paradises and hells, with subdivisions for Mormons and Southern Baptists. And the Jews who had an Orthodox heaven and a Reform one..."

"...and there were Brahmin paradises and ones for Sudras and Dalits..."

"...and Confucian afterlives, and Taoist immortals..."

"However, it wasn't all work and no fun. Sometimes we'd have a particularly pompous candidate who knew all the answers, could recite the *Koran* backwards, had been on pilgrimage twenty-five times...really walked the walk and prayed the pray...but was so self-confident that we'd decide to have a little fun with him, ask him what Allah's middle name was. Or ask, 'If a camel is four and a quarter meters long and each foot covers one and one-half meters in a regular step and if a camel caravan with fourteen camels leaves Damascus at 6:07 a.m. with each animal carrying 226 pounds of salt and flour, and if a caravan leaves Baghdad at 6:13 a.m. with thirty-one camels each carrying 187 pounds of sugar — at what hour and minute in how many days would they meet one another?'"

"Well, the candidate would start to stutter and fluster and tremble. We'd have a couple of Jinns thump up and down on the earth outside the grave, sort of earthquake-like. When we figured some of the theological conceit had worn off, we'd wave him on through. Allah never seemed to mind when we brought the proud down a step or two."

"But the Ecumenical Cruise changed all that..."

"Yes, that was all before the Ecumenical Cruise. Once that ecumenical proclamation got out, you know, proclaimed everywhere, you can imagine the panic...if all gods are equal, then all 'goods' are equal and all 'beliefs' are equally valid..."

"...and all paradises are the same and open to anyone who believes anything, no matter how bizarre...monkey-headed gods and giant cabbages had as much significance as Allah or Jehovah or Brahman or Vishnu, or the Kitchen God or Isis or Ishtar…"

"Given that state of affairs, was there any way that anyone who believed in anything…rivers, scorpions, birds, the wind…any way that anyone could be denied entrance to this universal paradise? That was when Allah suggested to the gods and goddesses that we, old Munkar and Nakir, based on our experiences with the two and seventy jarring sects should be named a committee of two for designing test questions that no matter what people believed would eliminate the undesirables and unbelievers…though it was not clear as to what sort of stuff people could unbelieve that would keep them out."

"The gods agreed, even those who had never heard of Islam, and we got the assignment. The only thing for sure was that atheists could not be admitted because they didn't believe in Paradise…but they didn't want in anyway and seemed content to die without please or squeeze."

"We tried to make up a list of questions…"

"We would ask 'Who is the prophet of Allah?' And the individual would respond that AT&T was up, but for long term there's more profit to be made in Japanese small cap stocks controlled by market Kammi on the Tokyo Stock Exchange. Or, 'Allah's profit is tied to hajj travel costs.' Or we would ask, you know making it kind of more general, 'Do you believe there is a god?' And a soul would respond, 'Sure, absolutely! She's in charge of fertility and blessed me with ten children before I switched religions and went for a little more asceticism and dry bread.' So, you can see…what was left? We could ask shoe size, or whether gods can build mountains over which they cannot jump, or how many Jinns does it take to make a Jinn and tonic…"

"Finally, we just threw the doors open! Whether people worshipped a consecrated biscuit, a humongous French fry, or were possessed by a divine foot fetish…everyone made it."

"And as word spread, it came to the point where in villages and cities around the world people began exiting the earth en mass, riding comets and turbocharged SUVs, or swimming in alcohol or other substances to heaven without paying taxes, rents, alimony, growing old…escaping the stress that had come with modern technology. In most of the world, too, Paradise was clearly better than endless struggles with drought, plague, poverty, and war. Even though religious wars had ended, struggles for oil and other resources persisted."

"Munkar and I just sat there at the door and watched them swarming in like geese heading south to avoid an Arctic winter. There's probably nothing so depressing as being an angel out of work. Occasionally we'd ask each other questions just to keep in practice: 'If a camel caravan leaves Damascus, and another leaves Cairo...' The only one enjoying the change seemed to be the earth, because everybody, or at least all the believers, were leaving, and, as she pointed out, they're the worst kind because they tend to justify their rape of the environment with divine commandments."

"Then the appeals from the nether regions started to pour in...'I was a Protestant sent to hell for blasphemy by the Roman Catholics.' 'I was a Jew, burned for my beliefs by Christians.' 'I was a Roman Catholic sent to hell for blasphemy by Protestants.' 'I was condemned as a Sikh, a Dalit, a Buddhist, a Shintoist, a Confucian...' 'I believed in Isis, Ishtar, Bogomil.' 'I crossed myself with two fingers instead of three and the Orthodox Church condemned me.' 'They sent me there because I married out of my caste, faith, village, race, political party, etc.' These too, retroactively, were also admitted, and pretty soon old Eblis himself sauntered up and noted as how he was enjoying the peace and quiet of the Underworld at last. Then armies of ancestors showed up...tired of being kept around, often in soggy rice paddies or steamy jungles, just to assure the prosperity of succeeding generations of their descendants for a couple of meal cakes a year and a stick of incense."

"In the beginning we didn't realize there were so many other gods. We saw only Allah and the two and seventy jarring sects and everybody else was 'Brand X' and didn't show up at our gate anyway. Now, as we sat there, we wondered about all those gods and spirits in a paradise that had begun to resemble a full monkey house with one banana...squeaks, screeches, yelling...even explosions! Apparently the explosions were caused by a group of 'paradisiacs' who were launching thunderbolts at competitive groups. Since they were now blessed with eternal life, the violence seemed to be turning into an end in itself."

"It became so bad that we couldn't sleep, even perched out there in the entry way with the gates three-quarters shut…and we wondered how the gods must be faring in that bedlam where it sounded like the paradisiacs had taken charge."

"…and we also started to wonder about all kinds of other things…like the origins of human beings in the first place. Every god and goddess from Tiamat to Prajapati to Nu Wa to Obatala to Jehovah to Allah claims he or she made them. We don't even know where we came from because they all insist they made us too way back when…"

"…and we began to wonder if the gods knew where they themselves came from…and did maybe human beings create the gods?"

"Well, it doesn't really make any difference because there we were, there the gods were, and there human beings were. And you and I had a job to do, or at least used to have a job to do."

"I suspect you're right, it doesn't make much difference who made whom now, after the Ecumenical Cruise."

"Finally, when no soul had appeared at the gates for almost a year, we began to assume that everyone had gone to Paradise who wanted to go, and we decided to close the great gates in order to shut in the noise. The doors hadn't been closed for a while, not since the Ecumenical Cruise, and they were stiff and squeaky and hard to move. Eblis came along to help and suggested that once we had them shut, we should take a well-deserved rest. With his help, we had just managed to get the doors almost shut when they were flung open again from inside and the three of us knocked down by a rush of hissing air!! At first we thought that the paradisiacs had figured out how to blow up Paradise itself. But then the rush of air repeated itself with a little less volume and we realized it was a 'Pssssst'."

"Right, the 'Psssss' of Allah, the 'sssst' of Jehovah…and there they both stood, Allah and Jehovah. This was the first time they'd come down together to check on us, because most of the time, they ran separate shows. The first thing we thought was it was going to be a 'soul audit'…that we'd let a rotten apple through. But the new arrangements where everybody who believed got in, made it difficult to figure out just what a rotten apple might be."

"It turned out that they weren't auditing, they were 'psssting' us because they wanted to slip out through the doors before we shut them, and they didn't want any of the other gods to know...and certainly didn't want the paradisiacs that now peopled Paradise to realize they were 'abandoning the ship' so to speak."

"They 'pssssted' one more time and whispered that they could not take the chaos any longer...the noise, the raucous laughter, the unending arguments of hordes of antagonistic souls all of whom now shared heavenly immortality. They wanted out!"

"Unfortunately, gods and goddesses have not really had much experience at whispering, so a divine whisper is like bang-up day in a salvage yard. No sooner had they explained to us their intent, than they were surrounded by a throng of other deities all of whom wanted the same thing...'out'. Siva was holding all four hands over his ears, Vulcan and Tiamat were hiccupping fiery little coughs. Jesus was holding Mary Magdalen by the hand, followed by Ishtar and Gilgamesh trying to slip around the edge of the crowd."

"You can imagine our consternation! Munkar and I, we were just doorkeepers, humble test proctors, and these were the gods abandoning the mob that now ran Paradise with the delicacy of angered wild elephants in a Hindu ashram."

"So, we left the doors open and the gods and goddesses in all their multifaceted forms and shapes flowed out, just as the tides of human souls had earlier swept in. The crawler gods crawled, the flyer gods flew, and those with extra arms helped those with no arms, so that in a matter of minutes it was all over. They were gone! But they needn't have worried about the paradisiacs wanting to leave heaven. The fireworks and yelling and screaming and noise of battle and distant lightning strikes continued unabated...intensified even...almost as though the flight of the gods and goddesses was a cause for celebration that at last it had become in heaven as it was on earth."

"At the doors it was now quiet, despite the awful racket in the distance. Just as we considered what we should do about the gates, Allah accompanied by Iza nagi and Horus came by and told us to close and lock them securely with the ancient key that stuck from the keyhole. We finally managed to close them, but turn the key we could not. It took all the combined strength of Munkar and I and

Iza nagi and Allah and Horus to make it turn. Then Allah removed the key and broke it in two and gave Munkar and me a half each to swallow so there would be no way of releasing back onto the earth the mobs of rampaging paradisiacs.

Crossing the Bridge

"What occurred then was an amazing reversal of that tide which had earlier swept in from the other direction across the Bridge of the Separator, passing through that Barzakh which divides the invisible and visible light spectrums. You see, the Bridge at its Paradise end is within the invisible and then at its midpoint passes through an invisible/visible light Barzakh into the visible that is the world. This division, as is the way of such separations, is neither the one nor the other nor both together. As the *Koran* says, it is like the dividing line between sweet and salt water or between light and shadow."

"At this light Barzakh the sphere of the things of heaven are separated from the things of earth. Every soul that has ever ascended into Paradise has crossed this Bridge, whether that soul awaited a Sumerian, Hindu, or Yoruba version of heaven on the other side. The soul passing over into Paradise leaves on the world side all the visible shapes and forms of its life and deeds."

"Earlier, Munkar and I, like other angels and gods, from Gabriel to the Stove God shuffling each year back to his Chinese hearth after having tattled on the homeowners to the Jade Emperor…all of us avoided the Bridge with its Barzakh and remained within the invisible light spectrum until we encountered those who were supposed to see us when we visited souls in their graves. We were visible only to the soul peeping through body's shutters. There were exceptions, of course, cases where angels passed through the Barzakh with their hearts and minds more on the 'daughters of men' than upon the possibility of returning once they had passed through. These exceptions were the origin of the 'giants on the earth in those days' stories in most religions…angels, gods, spirits who did not return through the Barzakh."

"But now, the tide of divinities and spirits had flooded across the Bridge and through the Barzakh as though deliberately emphasizing their total escape from Paradise and the paradisiacs.

Singly, in pairs, and in groups they had crossed. Hanuman and Sun Wu'-k'ung arm in arm with their tails entwined. Ishtar pulling Gilgamesh along by the hand. Jesus carrying Mary Magdalen in his arms. Crawling snake gods crawled, flying bird gods flew…all passing through the Barzakh where they became invisible to Nakir and I and Allah and Horus and Iza nagi waiting to close the gates after the last deity had left."

"Once the gates were shut and locked, our little group too moved on…"

"…and we were absolutely stunned by what we saw when we crossed over the Bridge and passed through the Barzakh!"

"There before us were piles and mounds and mountains of abandoned shapes and masks and body parts – not of human beings, but of the retreating gods! It was as though an army fleeing a field of battle had tossed everything that could encumber it, everything not essential!"

"It was bizarre and comical at the same time. There were stacks of arms and hands and legs…probably of Hindu and indigenous tribal deities. There were the two extra heads and six arms of No Zha tossed on a heap of centaur parts and horns and tusks. Suits of armor and helmets of every age and place from the bushy feathered plumes of Aztec sky gods to the polished plate of Mars and Thor. On the top of one such pile were the tails of Hanuman and Sun Wu-k'ung, still entwined. Extra eyes and ears were scattered about like marbles. To one side we saw the trunk complete with tusks and giant ears of Ganesha. Demeter's horse head with bit and bridle still in it, other beasts' heads, tails, hooves, horns, giant penises, claws, and beaks…"

"On another pile rested the limp form of Osiris and we assumed he had been slain until we realized he must have been but a part of Isis which she had now shed."

"Interestingly, in all these mounds of parts there was no sign of blood, no sign of violence. When Horus turned to us to remark upon this fact, as he opened his beak to speak his entire hawk's head fell off!"

"Actually, 'fell off' isn't quite correct…more like it was sloughed off as a snake or a cicada sloughs its old skin to reveal the new. Immediately beneath the splitting hawk's 'mask' there emerged the face of a dark-complexioned young man, a face completely framed in shiny black curls."

"It was this way all along the Bridge and the road on the other side…as if all these gods and spirits had started life as human beings, men and women, and were now returning to their natural state, shedding the forms and body parts and symbols that had been impressed upon them through the centuries. And these body parts and masks even as we proceeded were dissolving and disappearing so that only a fine dust remained."

"It happened to us too, to Munkar and I, those little leathery brown wings we had used to scout about the earth dropped off and disintegrated even before they touched the ground."

"The Jade Emperor's peacock feather and jade cloak vanished leaving him in hempen breeches and rice straw sandals. Most interesting of all was the transformation of Jehovah and Allah. Both had bald patches, but where Jehovah's began over his forehead and swept backward, Allah's was at the back of his head and swept forward. Where Jehovah had a wart on his left cheek and a dimple on the right, Allah had a wart on his right cheek and a dimple on his left. Allah had a slight tic in his right eye, Jehovah had a tic in his left. Jehovah was left-handed and gestured with this left hand when he spoke, Allah was right-handed and gesticulated with his right when he spoke. When Allah walked, his left foot toed in slightly, whereas with Jehovah the right did so. Both had long black and gray, neatly trimmed beards that were indistinguishable from one another. It was as though they were copies of one another. One was the positive and the other was the negative and vice versa. Both were rounded out and wrinkled up with middle-age spreads. Allah's appeared above the belt line of his loose-hung silk trousers, Jehovah's below the belt line."

"Near this set of 'twins', a pensive Zeus was contemplating the fragments of steer hide and blowing feathers which were all that remained of his disguises. Beside him stood Indra wrapped in the remnants of a tattered cat skin and up to his kneecaps in the thousand and one vaginas with which the muni Gautama had decorated him as punishment for adultery…"

"…and our once black dreadlocks had silvered!"

"This procession of retreating gods resembled a mass of ornately decorated Christmas trees liberated from their holders and marching away, de-decorating themselves as they went...tossing tinsel, glass, artificial snow, and colored lights...everything...until only the simple green branches and stems were left of all that which had been so elaborately disguised."

"We also wondered if, having passed through the Barzakh, it would be possible for us to return if we coughed up the key. Actually, apart from a few exceptions, most of the gods, I believe, really did not want to go back after they had adjusted to being men and women among people who did not believe in their divine nature, but who did accept them as fellows. Siva could wear pants with two pockets. Ganesha could brush his teeth without stabbing himself on his tusks, or comb his hair without catching his ears in the comb. And as Horus said, at last he was able to kick the gravel and grit habit. I think Ahura Mazda put it best when he said that when one is in Paradise, one forgets the beauty of earth's sunrises and sunsets, the majesty of her sand and sea storms, and the infinite variety of her landscapes and seasons...but most of all one forgets the peace and quiet of her empty places...."

"Oh, some of them certainly missed the grandeur of earlier days. Armies marching off to slaughter one another in a deity's name. But on the other hand, now that they seemed to have returned to their human roots, and the layers of heads and arms and attributes and animal parts had dropped off and disappeared, most of them seemed relieved. Still, for some the adjustments that followed were not easy."

"That's the way it's been since. Heaven's full of Muslims, Taoists, Hindus, Jews, Christians, and an infinite mix of indigenous polytheists, pantheists, and animists of every sort. In fact many areas of Africa, the South Pacific, and Kansas were largely uninhabited for years as the non-believers in these areas were few in those days, and vastly outnumbered by the believers who early saw this open trip to immortality and eternal paradise as a wonderful escape from the taxes, corruption, poverty, alcoholism, exploitation, disease, ethnic violence, and big government that plagued their short lives."

"A grand paradox isn't it? Paradise was full of saints and prophets and gurus and medicine folk and priests...the Muslims gathered about Mohammed trying to get him to repudiate other Muslims, the Christians tugging the Apostles around by their beards to get them to side with Catholics, Protestants, Copts, Orthodox Greeks, and Slavs in endless theological debates. The Saivas quarreling with the Vaisnavas over the place and position of the now-departed Siva and Vishnu. Mideastern struggles among revealed religions now occur daily on the streets of Paradise, but without the gods. Muslims but no Allah. Jews but no Jehovah. Christians but no Jesus. The visible world full of gods and no believers, and Paradise full of believers and no gods! "

"Down here the atheists and non-believers have all the gods and yet believe in none of them while the paradisiacs have Paul, apostles, popes, martyrs, Luther, Augustine, Aquinas, Al-Arabi, Maimonides, rabbis…reform, orthodox, orthodox-reform-…but no Jehovah…"

"…and sadhus, pandits, gurus, brahmins, Ramakrishna, Vivekenanda, Sankara, Ramanujan, but no Krishna or Brahman…"

"Although, as Eblis suggested, and he seems to have his avenues of information, the paradisiacs in no way missed the patron deities of their systems and were in fact thriving without them…on the other hand, some of the gods and spirits that we've encountered in our wanderings had to make some very difficult adjustments."

"It wasn't just that each had ceased to be the center of a 'belief universe', the central sun or star in it…no, when the gods entered the world of non-believers, they lost not only their attributes but also all the meaning aspects that human beings had given them, both physical forms and emotional characteristics. In one sense, this was probably good and most of them felt relieved to be beyond reputations of 'angry, vengeful, fearsome, hateful, warlike'…constantly on call to participate in the petty squabbles of their worshippers. Even the 'ever watchful eye' business was a relief when it 'shut' so that they could get a good night's sleep and enjoy a laid-back cappuccino in a plaza de something or other."

"But imagine millennia of being the 'meaning source' for human existence and the justification, even the aider and abetter, of every good as well as every foul and violent act, always held responsible for justifying the torture, pain, and mystic fraud of their devotees and their leaders, providing meaning to the meaningless…to suddenly find that as provider of meaning, your own being has become meaningless."

"Some gods were younger than others. Some were as old as certain kinds of speculations about human origins. All of them were now men and women among unbelievers who were also men and woman, and who had nothing against giving them jobs, inviting them in for tea, even asking them for advice…and many of these newcomers seemed quite wise. In fact, it was this 'wisdom' which some of them brought that led them into professions of different sorts. Jesus and Mary, who later had a little girl and a little boy, went in for marriage counseling and family planning…which was simpler, like so many things that were now considered human matters, unclouded with appeals to the whys and wherefores and whims of a set of deities. Nu Wa, Isis, and Ishtar joined the 'human liberation movement', which worked internationally to remove the dark vestiges of injustice, inequality, and slavery of races and genders. Fortunately, those who had seen such inequalities as originating with the will of the gods were snugly settled in Paradise arguing eternally with other paradisiacs."

"Of course, strife and conflict didn't go away on earth just because those who used to ask the gods for support and justification for their positions, no matter how bizarre, had gone to Paradise. No, but what was different was that justifications occurred in and on human terms. Somehow genocide was harder to sell if its justification was nothing more than greed and jealousy, just as institutions like slavery and oppression of women and exploitation of children seemed less justifiable when all one could say was 'just because' and not that this god or that god made some folk to be slaves and other folk to be masters…or made some to be priests and others to be choirboys."

"We too were relieved after it was all over. We got our teeth cleaned, haircuts…dreadlocks get to be terribly dirty and stiff after a thousand years or so and it's hard to make them behave. And we both learned to ski."

"That's right, ski! It seemed to us that it would be wonderful, gliding over the snow like we used to glide with our stubby, brown wings in an updraft on a hot day. Besides, skiing enabled us to get close on the high Alpine slopes to the Bridge every year at winter solstice to listen whether there was more or less noise…"

"In time there did seem to be less, although Paradise still echoed like a three-wheeled cart full of cymbal players in endless practice traveling down a rocky mountain trail at great speed."

"Gradually in our lifetime here, Munkar's and mine, the world seems to have become a happier place in which life begins at birth and ends at death…a continuum with infinite high and low points between beginning and ending. And the recognition of this seems to encourage an empathy among human beings who recognize that they share this continuum with one another…and the gods who recognize that it applies to them as well for they have seen so many of their once-divine colleagues return to the earth from which they came. Jehovah no longer has to stand on his fierceness and jealousies. He and Allah can concentrate their efforts as civil engineers upon making Baghdad and Jerusalem healthier places with new sewage systems."

"Some gods it is true never really adjusted. They could be found lurking in the entry ways to their temples and holy places, which were now museums, hospitals, and libraries…as though waiting for some kind of 'return to glory'. Others were unhappy until they located jobs that seemed remarkably similar to their activities as gods. Huitzsilopochtli, the Aztec sun god, experienced extended periods of 'sacrifice withdrawal syndrome' until he finally found a job in a Tuscan slaughterhouse where with Mars he worked the day shift while his sister Coyolyauhguit and Kali worked the night shift. Indra and Zeus made a successful living from the sale of vitamin and mineral supplements to increase human male hormonal functions and to retard female aging. Krishna became security director at an international airport where his followers had earlier harassed passengers. Iza nami not only broke through the glass ceiling at IBM, she shattered it completely. Obatala, before his passing, refitted one of the Christian Brothers wineries in California and made it a world distribution center for Obatala brand 'Palm Cooler'."

"With few exceptions, no matter what else they did, most of the gods were committed to improving the environment and stopping its destruction now that it was their home again. As Jehovah explained to us one day, there was a deep and abiding guilt in most of their hearts for the terrible things that were done in and justified in their names to poor old earth."

"We used to see most of the gods once in a while and every year a dwindling group of us would get together to ski in the Alps near the spot where the Bridge once ended. Of course there are no traces on the high slopes any more. But most of us who gathered there at winter solstice could usually hear the party proceeding unabated, though fading in volume…at least until recently. Incidentally, it was from Eblis that we learned that the paradisiacs must have somehow managed to free Paradise from its earthly mooring points and so it is beginning to drift off through the infinite universe…a closed and cosmic party."

"I remember that just before we finally got the gates closed, Gabriel and a group of Sumerian angels that he spent a lot of time with came by. And when they saw the last of the gods had left, most of them about-faced and flew off in the other direction. Only Gabriel remained and urged us as 'an old friend' to come on back in 'now that there would be a more festive mood in the place'. We thanked him of course…he was always kindly disposed to us and chatted with us when no one else would."

"'Well,' he said, 'You might want to reconsider, because this is the big one you know…eternity, immortality, and an endless supply of all the good things that Paradise can offer the paradisiac even if the human race wipes itself out down below…besides I don't think there will be any second chances.'"

"He said something else about the 'gods going home' which we didn't understand at the time. When we politely refused, he brought out a bottle of something or other and asked us to drink a farewell toast with him, 'To heaven, may it ever remain as it was on earth!' We broke our glasses against a cloud bank and he flew back to Paradise and the paradisiacs."

"After we got the doors closed, we never saw Gabriel or any of the other heavenly host again. Eblis, who was the only other angel to leave, suggested to us one time that this was the true 'revolt of the angels' and that Gabriel and others had been planning it for a long time, even conducting secret experiments with methane gas. But Eblis is full of himself sometimes and he never did like Gabriel."

"Ah well, I guess it is true though, as Eblis has suggested, that the paradisiacs have managed to free Paradise from its moorings, because for the last two years at winter solstice when we approached the highest point on the passes the sounds seemed to come from farther and farther away."

"On the other hand, it might not have anything to do with Paradise drifting, and everything to do with our hearing. All of us, gods, Munkar and I and Eblis, we have not only lost our immortality, we're all losing our hearing. It goes with aging. Our hair is gray and falling out. Where Krishna's and Horus's locks were once virile curl jungles, they now fringe like snow their icy pools of bald pates. Jehovah and Allah and Iza nagi are completely bald and stooping badly...and I admit that seeing them now in their bathing trunks on the beaches of Abu Al Aqabah is always kind of startling. Some gods have married the sons and daughters of human beings...no giants this time. Only kids like kids have always been. Jesus and Mary for example already have grandchildren. Vishnu sired over twenty children in three marriages before he left us. We ourselves never thought much about marriage. I guess, like Eblis, we are confirmed bachelors who share a game of cards Tuesday evenings, a walk on Sundays, and winter ski outings as often as we can afford them...and of course our annual pilgrimage to the Alpine slopes to listen for a while and then later in a lodge in front of a warm fire reminisce about the world before the Ecumenical Cruise, and gossip about who is still with us and who is gone."

And this is where I first met them a number of years ago in a Tyrolean ski lodge above Bolzano, and where I last saw them three years ago at winter solstice. I have often tried to hear the sounds of Paradise that they talked about, but have never succeeded. Perhaps Eblis was right, the paradisiacs have managed to free the corners of the cosmic party and it has already drifted beyond our galaxy. In the crowded cities of the world I have also tried to catch glimpses of the gods before they are all gone. Munkar and Nakir always refused to point them out to me when we talked and I would ask. Now when

I catch sight of an aging figure on the street or in a sidewalk café, I wonder if this could be Isis or Demeter or Allah or Brahman or the Jade Emperor. But just as I get my courage up to ask, the old man or woman hacks and coughs or plumbs an ear hole with a little finger, and then I stop and think, "No, no god would do that!"

Notes

Queen Vashti Goes to Heaven

1. Heinrich Kramer and James Sprenger, *The Malleus Maleficarum* (New York: Dover Publications, 1978) p. 44.

2. Mohammed Marmaduke Pickthall, *The Meaning of the Glorious Koran* (New York: Mentor Religious Classics/ The New American Library, 1963) p. 83.

3. Ibid, p. 306.

4. Aristotle, *Generation of Animals*, trans. and ed. A. L. Peck (Cambridge: Harvard University Press, 1957) Vol. I, xx, pp. 170-171.

5. *The Laws of Manu* ix, trans. Georg Buehler, in *The Sacred Books of the East*, vol. XXV (New York: Dover Publications reprint, 1969) p. 330.

6. *Blindfold Jataka*, trans. and ed. Caroline A. F. Rhys Davis, in *Stories of the Buddha, Being Selections fom the Jataka*, (New York: Dover Publications reprint, 1989) p. 67.

7. *Gospel according to Thomas*, in Jean Doresse, *The Secred Books of the Egyptian Gnostics* (New York: Viking, 1960) p. 234.

The Cup of Coffee

1. *Great Sanskrit Plays In Modern Translation*, trans. P. Lal (New York: New Directions Books, 1964) p. 82.

Satori at the Doughnut Stop

1. Philip Wheelwright, "Parmenides," in *The Presocratics* (New York: Prentice Hall, 1966) p. 97.

2. David J. Kalupahana, *Nagarjuna: The Philosophy of the Middle Way*, (Buffalo: SUNY Press, 1986) p. 269.

3. Nicholas of Cusa, *The Vision of God*, trans. E. G. Salter (New York: E.P. Dutton, 1928) p. 47.

Helen Morley's Finger

1. *The Book of Lieh-tzu* , trans. A. C. Graham (New York: Columbia University Press, 1990) p. 67.

Metamorphosis

1. H. C. Warren, *Buddhism in Translation* (New York: Atheneum, 1963) p. 146.

2. *Jaina Sutras, Parts I and II*, trans. Herman Jacobi (New Delhi: Motilal Banarsidass, 1980) Part I, p. 11.

Christians and Buddhists at Winter Solstice

1. Arthur W. Ryder, *The Panchatantra* (Chicago: University of Chicago Press, 1956) p. 24.

2. "Patika Sutta," in *Digha Nikaya (The Long Discourses of the Buddha)*, trans. Maurice Walshe (Boston: Wisdom Publications, 1995) pp. 378-9.

3. Jean Doresse, *The Secret Books of the Egyptian Gnostics* (New York: Viking Press, 1960) p. 356.

4. *Menander, The Principal Fragments*, trans. Francis G. Allinson (Cambridge: Loeb Classical Library, Harvard University Press reprint, 1959) p. 177.

5. Eusebius, *Life of Constantine*, trans. Averil Cameron and Stuart G. Hall (Oxford: Clarendon Ancient History Series, Oxford University Press, 1999) pp. 80-82.

History and Development of Modern Flap Techniques

1. *The Laws of Manu*, trans. Georg Buehler, in *The Sacred Books of the East*, vol. XXV (New York: Dover Publications reprint, 1969) p. 166.

2. "Katha," in *The Upanishads*, trans. Swami Prabhavanda and Frederick Manchester (New York: Mentor Relgious Classics, 1957) p. 20.

When Siva Lost His Cool

1. Joseph Francois Michaud, *History of the Crusades* (New York: A. C. Armstrong, 1881) vol. I, pp. 50-52.

2. *The Meaning of the Glorious Koran*, trans. Mohammed Marmaduke Pickthal (New York: Mentor Religious Classics, The New American Library, 1963) Surah IX, pp. 148-9.

3. Ibid, Surah IV, pp. 74-77.

4. Ibid, Surah II, pp. 190-91.

The Zoo

[1] Pliny the Elder, *Natural History*, trans. H. Rackham (Cambridge: Harvard University Press, 1950) BK VII iii 30, vol II, pp. 525-7.

.

The Making of Presidents

1. Aristotle, *The Works of Aristotle, De Partibus Animalium*, trans. William Ogle (Oxford: The Clarendon Press, 1912) pp. 652-653

Passover in the English Department

1. *The Laws of Manu*, trans. Georg Buehler, in *The Sacred Books of the East*, vol. XXV (New York: Dover Publications reprint, 1969) pp. 65-67.

Miracle with a Moral

1. *Gilgamesh*, trans. John Gardner and John Maier (New York: Vintage Books, 1984) pp. 249-50.

2. *The Lost Books of the Bible, Being All the Gospels, Epistles, and Other Pieces Now Extant Attributed in the First Four Centuries to Jesus Christ, His Apostles and Their Companions* (Cleveland: World Publishing Co., 1929; reprint, New York: Bell Publishing Company, 1979) pp. 38-60.

The Man Who Worked at Crunchy's

1. *The Presocratics*, ed. Phillip Wheelwright (New York: Macmillan, 1966) p. 185.

2. Wint-tsit Chan, "The Analects of Confucius," in *A Source Book in Chinese Philosophy* (Princeton: Princeton University Press, 1973) p. 22.

3. *The Laws of Manu*, trans. George Buehler, in *The Sacred Books of the East*, vol. XXV (New York: Dover Publications reprint, 1969) p. 199.

In Therapy

1. *The Vedanta Sutras of Badarayana, With the Commentary of Sankara*, trans. George Thibaut, vol. I (New York: Dover Publications, 1962) pp. 3-4.

The Bed Bug

1. *The Gulistan of Sa'di*, trans. Edward Rehatsek (New York: Capricorn Books, 1966) p. 139.

2. *The Panchatantra*, trans. Arthur W. Ryder (Chicago: University of Chicago Press, 1956) p. 320.

The Second Coming

1. W. G. Lambert, "The Poem of the Righteous Sufferer," in *Babylonian Wisdom Literature* (London: Oxford Univeristy Press, 1960) pp. 41-43.

The Ecumenical Cruise

1. Louis Ginzberg, *The Legends of the Jews*, trans. Henrietta Szold, vol. I (Philadelphia: The Jewish Publication Society of America, 1968) pp. 34-35.

2. *The Presocratics*, ed. Philip Wheelwright (New York: Macmillan, 1966) pp. 32-33.

3. *The Laws of Manu*, xi:85, trans. Georg Buehler, in *The Sacred Books of the East*, vol. XXV (New York: Dover Publications reprint, 1969) p. 447.

4. *Gilgamesh*, trans. John Gardner and John Maier (New York: Vintage Books, 1985) Tablet xi, column iv, pp. 239-41.

5. *Matthew* 18:18.

6. Imam-I-A'zam Abu Hanifa, *Belief and Islam* (Istanbul: Waqf Publications No. 8, 1995) p. 65.

7. Louis Ginzberg, *The Legends of the Jews*, trans. Henrietta Szold, vol. I (Philadelphia: The Jewish Publication Society of America, 1968) pp. 124-5.

8. H. A. R. Gibb and J. H. Kramers, *The Shorter Encyclopaedia of Islam* (Ithaca: Cornell University Press, 1953) p. 59.